what Happened to cass McBride?

a novel by Gail Giles

LITTLE, BROWN AND COMPANY

New York ⚭ Boston

Little, Brown and Company

Hachette Book Group USA
237 Park Avenue, New York, NY 10017
Visit our Web site at www.lb-teens.com

First Paperback Edition: May 2007
First published in hardcover in 2006 by Little, Brown and Company

The characters and events portrayed in this book are fictitious. Any similarity to real persons, living or dead, is coincidental and not intended by the author.

The author wishes to acknowledge www.mamalisa.com for the lyrics to "Front, petit front."

Library of Congress Cataloging-in-Publication Data

Giles, Gail.
  What happened to Cass McBride? / by Gail Giles.— 1st ed.
     p. cm.
  Summary: After his younger brother commits suicide, Kyle Kirby decides to exact revenge on the person he holds responsible.
  ISBN-13: 978-0-316-16638-6 (hardcover)
  ISBN-10: 0-316-16638-3 (hardcover)
  ISBN-10: 0-316-16639-1 (paperback)
  ISBN-13: 978-0-316-16639-3 (paperback)
  [1. Revenge — Fiction. 2. Suicide — Fiction. 3. Crime — Fiction. 4. Family problems — Fiction.] I. Title.
PZ7.G3923Wh 2006
[Fic] — dc22

                                        2005037298

HC 10 9 8 7 6 5 4 3 2 1
PB 10 9 8 7 6 5 4 3

RRD-C

Printed in the United States of America
Cover photograph by Lisa Bowe
Book design by Tracy Shaw

The text was set in Charlotte Sans, Mrs. Eaves, and Agfa Rotis, and the display type is Platelet and Orange.

Always and always and always for Jim Giles and Josh Jakubik,
My heroes — G.G.

KYLE

"She's dead, isn't she? If she was alive, I wouldn't be handcuffed to a table in an interview room. You'd take her statement before you'd come at me for a confession, right?"

The big cop, the older one that looked like he could still play a mean game of hoops if he didn't have to run much, didn't change expression. Arms crossed over his chest, he just waited me out. I shrugged. I was in such deep shit that I guess it didn't make much difference if Cass McBride was dead or not. She did what she did and she got what she deserved. Maybe she was collateral damage, but that mouth of hers put her in the strike zone.

"So, I talk straight into the camera? You'll let me tell the story how I want? I won't tell you shit unless all of it gets out there. In the papers and on the news. I want people to know. I want the gossip to chew on *her* for a while. You get that, don't you?"

I turned away from the camera. Closed my eyes. David's face swam on the back of my eyelids.

"Kyle? You still with us?"

Knee-jerk reaction. I shifted my glance to the young cop, with last year's hair. I dug my index fingers into the sides of my thumbs at the cuticle until the pain chased David out of my head.

"Dude, your thumbs are bleeding," the young cop said.

I slid my sleeves down and covered my hands. "If you can't see it, it's not there. *Dude.*" Both the cops lifted their chins at my display of 'tude. Tough shit. I don't like it if somebody sees me bleed.

"My timeline is a little sketchy," I said. "Today's what? Sunday?" David's funeral was Friday, so I thought it'd been a couple of days.

A little red light blinked on the camera. I scratched the back of my neck with my covered knuckles then stared down the lens.

"Yes, it's Sunday, well . . ." The big cop looked at

his wristwatch. "No, it's Monday morning. But take us back to what happened on Friday. Can you tell me how you picked the place?"

"That was the easy part. I work for the people that own the place. There's a main house and a separate guesthouse that the owners only use in winter. It's vacant now and I keep the lawn mowed. They had me paint the bottom panes of the greenhouse and use it to store the pool supplies and lawn stuff. It has a dirt floor. It was the perfect place."

CASS

David Kirby's funeral was this morning. I didn't go. It would look beyond strange if I did.

I wasn't sure he'd . . . *done* what he did because of that stupid note. I wish I hadn't left it lying around. Well, I wish I hadn't written it.

But I guess David didn't show it to anyone. Threw it away or burned it maybe?

I had one of those wild-monkeys-fighting-over - a - banana - inside - your - cranium headaches from worrying about it. I waited for Dad to go to bed then prowled his briefcase. He always had Xanax in there. Score. I took one. Then went back for another. This was two-Xan stress.

I took a long, hot shower, setting the pulsing jets of water on *masochist* and stood so it could drum the back of my neck and shoulders. I rolled my head as the steam swirled around and the water sluiced over me. *The pills might be kicking in.* An empty stomach was a welcoming friend to drugs. Thank the Lord Dad was a hypocrite. While he preached to me, he sure didn't say no to online rip-off pharmacies. Hallelujah.

Drugs definitely kicking in. I'd gone gospel in the shower. I got out and toweled off. I blow-dried my hair until it was damp thirty. My hair was dry enough so I slid into my nightclothes, pulled back the covers, and nestled in.

I watched the play of the lamplight from the end of my fingers. Nice. *Drugs can make the simplest thing so entertaining.* I switched the lamp off and settled into the drug drowse. Deep breath. *No dreams, Cass. No trees. No ropes. No notes. No boys with big ears. Nothing.*

BEN

At ten fifteen Saturday morning the lieutenant ripped a page out of his notebook and slapped it on Detective Ben Gray's desk. "Possible missing kid in Sterling Meadows. Roger Oakley's first on scene. Says we need a look."

"How old is the kid?" Ben asked.

"Roger says seventeen, but says he's almost positive it's not a case of party hearty and too loaded to make it home."

Ben nodded. "Go ahead and call Crime Scene out. Roger's good. He wouldn't put out a squawk unless he's got something for us."

"Yeah, says he's pretty sure she was snatched from the house."

Ben's left eyebrow shot up. He grabbed his jacket from the back of his chair and called to his partner. "Scott, let's roll. Let's find out what happened to . . ." He glanced down at the notepaper. "Cass McBride."

KYLE

"Did you have things set up at the greenhouse before you took her?" the big cop asked me, looking confused.

I was tired. And this was going to take forever if the cop was totally stupid. Or maybe he was establishing premeditation.

"Sure, everything was ready before the funeral. The pump, the box, everything." The cops exchanged glances. Fine. Like a crime like this could happen accidentally.

"Go ahead. Did she wake up in your truck or what?" This was from the young cop.

"She took forever to wake up. She worried me because her breathing was so . . ." I stopped. "I had to put my ear to her chest to check if her heart was beating. I didn't know that much about the drug I gave her. And she was really limp."

My mind spun off and I wondered if David was limp when they took him down from that tree.

"I can't."

"Sure you can, David. It's what eight-year-old boys do. It's time for you to climb that tree."

"This one is too hard. There's no low branches. I can't reach."

"That's why it's fun. Always set your sights high. Pick something just out of reach. It's not fun if it's too easy," I said. I leaned down to him. "Here's how it works. You just see it happening in your head. Then get back and run at the tree. Hit it with your left foot then your right like you're running straight up, then jump for the branch. It'll be above your head, but you'll have momentum. After that you can go from limb to limb easy."

I looked down at the table, dug into my thumbs again. Stay in the now, I told myself. Don't lose it yet. You can pay for your part in this later. Back to the lens.

"In the greenhouse there was some moonlight," I said, "but I had a flashlight and when I laid it on the ground, it was surreal. A film noir director would get off on it." I saw the young, snotty cop kind of roll up his eyes.

"You don't think I know film noir?" I shot at him. "You think I'm a Cro-Magnon, with a walnut brain? Live in my world for a while and you'll know what *noir* really is. I read too. Books without pictures. With long words. What about you, still hung up on *Maxim*?"

The big cop gave a half-shake of his head, a signal for me to keep on task and for the snotty cop to let it go.

"Like I was saying. It was surreal. This rag-doll girl in white pj's caught in moonlight and one bright shaft of light across her face and me standing over her."

I looked up and saw that the big cop finally changed expression. He looked at me the way *she* would look at David. As something less than human.

I caught the camera lens like it was an eye. "It was quiet." I jabbed at the lens with a pointed finger. "You don't know how I like the quiet. I don't get much of it. It's a luxury.

"I checked Cass. She was alive, just out. I remember

thinking how warm and soft she was when I picked her up and how innocent evil could look when sleeping."

I stared at my hands. My right was cuffed to a ring welded to the tabletop. "I hung around for a few hours, but needed to be home by morning, so I bailed.

"Figured maybe it would be better if Cass woke up when I was gone. I wanted her to lose her goddamn cool and go apeshit trying to figure out where she was. Then I'd start the torture."

CASS

A mojo headache kicked my temples, dragging me up toward realworld. Last night's weird-ass dream left me stiff and I hurt all over. I rocked my head, trying to get the ache in my neck to back the hell off, then arched my back and stretched my toes.

Wrong. And wronger. No twelve-hundred count cotton sheets against bare toes. Something hard and rough. Like wood. Splintery wood. And a sound. Kind of a thumping. My head throbbed, fuzzy and thick, as the headache amped up. Was I hearing my own head pound? Xanax had never given me a headache. Never had one like this.

Did I grab something else in Dad's briefcase? Was my father into X now? Was this a hallucination?

I opened my eyes. Nothing. Dark. Blind dark.

Were my eyes open? This headache? Was I batshit blind? I smelled urine. Strong, and oh, god, I was wet. What the hell? My hands jerked, banged a rough surface above, then collided with my face. I couldn't see them. Something heavy smacked my head. My right hand. It was wrong. Heavy. Encased in . . . or . . . fixed to a block? That's what hit my head. What the hell?

I hurt like I'd fallen down the stairs and my head was woozy and I couldn't move or see and my right hand was all wadded up. *Accident!* Had I been in an accident? Was I all bandaged up or . . .

My left hand traveled the surface of the thing fixed to my hand. Rectangle. Smallish. Square button left open, ready for my thumb. Too big for a pager. Not a cell phone, not enough buttons. A radio? One of those two-way things? Why? Maybe a hospital? One of those call button things taped to my hand? But it was too big. Way too big. And there was too much tape around it. No, not a hospital.

I felt my eyes. They were open. I wasn't blindfolded, but was I blind? I closed my eyes. Opened them. Was there any difference? Fuck if I knew.

Please be a dream. I hope I took X. Anything but this being real.

I pulled my feet in and my knees knocked a surface. Pushed my arms and hands out. Raised my hands up again.

Rough wood. Little more than shoulder width. Maybe a foot longer than my height. Dear god, no more than twelve inches above as I lay flat. I whimpered. I started rocking slightly back and forth as panic set in.

That weird dream I had. There was a sound. Almost musical. Piano keys all struck at once. Or maybe glass? And then the breeze. Like an open window. A thumping sound.

My head was unfocused but this wasn't a dream. I wasn't in my bed or a hospital. Fear clutched me hard. My stomach roiled. And I thought maybe I knew how it feels come heart attack time. Because mine actually squeezed. Just squeezed into a hard knot and burned. I felt it release. I gasped and the tears came complete with a sob and shivers.

I was chilled. Not cold. But, yes, chilled was

the right word, like a glass from the fridge, kind of damp, and . . .

The smell. That was what had been creeping in on me. Not just the urine. Something damp and . . . earthy.

Where was I? Why? I was trapped in something small and dark and wet and . . .

I sucked in and screamed.

I screamed until I felt like the blood vessels in my face and neck would burst. I screamed until my throat felt ripped, shredded, and I banged and kicked until my hands and heels and toes had to be as shredded as my throat.

You scream when you want someone to come.

Someone did.

Oh dear god. Someone did.

BEN

Ben Gray wasn't. He was black. That was his joke. Even he was tired of it, though. Basketball scholarship, but not talented enough for the pros. Ben loved his job, but knew not to live it. His partner didn't know that yet. Scott Michaels's shield was shiny new and his energy was exhausting. He had spiked hair, for god's sake, looked like a surfer, and acted like a cocker spaniel on speed.

"Roger Oakley," Ben said. "Never screws up. If the family hasn't messed up the place, we're in great shape."

"You think we got an Amber?"

Ben sighed. "We don't go in guessing."

"I know. But this would be my first Amber."

"Scott," Ben said, his tone a warning.

"I know. Don't say Amber again."

The subdivision where Cass McBride lived was gated but without a guard. Ben pressed the code Roger had given him and the gate opened. As his rat's-back-brown Crown Vic crawled through, Ben noted that the car behind him rolled in on his tail. Well, he thought, it was better than no security at all, but not much.

A man in pajama bottoms and a T-shirt, his hair sticking up in tufts, waited on the porch with Officers Roger Oakley and Tyrell Ford.

The man in pajamas started talking as soon as Ben stepped onto the porch.

"I didn't touch anything," the distraught man said. "When I saw the glass I knew not to. I just backed out of the room and called. I told these guys that."

Ben shot a glance at Roger. "Oakley. Glad to hear you caught this one."

Roger nodded. Compliment received. "This is Ted McBride."

"Cass would never run away," Mr. McBride said, leaning forward and jabbing the air with a pointed finger. "Understand that. Go look at that glass. Someone took my girl."

"I hear you, Mr. McBride. We're here to get your daughter back as soon as possible. Why don't we go in the house?"

Ben's eyebrow registered the word "glass" as why he and Scott had been called out. Roger had gotten a case of his legendary "spider feet," when he felt like spiders were racing up his neck. Something was wrong in this house.

Before Ben could ask Ted another question, the man collapsed onto a couch and sobbed. He covered his face but tears leaked between his fingers and his attempts to muffle his sobs came out as rough coughs.

"She's my little girl. I'll give all this away to get her back." He began rocking back and forth. "Don't let her be hurt. Please."

Roger's partner, Tyrell, held up a small spiral notebook and pointed to the hall. He read in a low voice. "Father, Ted McBride, owner of the home. Mother lives in Louisiana. Divorced. Daughter, Cass McBride, 17, high school junior. Father and daughter home last night. Daughter went to her bedroom first. She wasn't up when he awoke. Went to check. She was missing. He saw broken glass on her floor. Immediately called police."

"Good work, Officer Ford."

They returned to the living room. McBride was sitting with forearms on knees, head hanging.

"Mr. McBride, I'm Detective Ben Gray and I'll be taking the lead on your daughter's case."

Ted swallowed hard then stood and shook Ben's hand. "Sorry about that. Ted McBride is a man that takes control. Ted McBride knows how things work, how to get things done. I have no idea where all that came from."

"Grief and fear, sir. Natural emotions in this situation."

"I disagree. Fear gets in the way and grief is premature. Cass is alive and I want her back. Emotions won't get her back. Work will."

Roger's spiders must have jumped over to Ben's neck. He could feel their feet. Was this guy having a breakdown? Talking about himself in the third person? "Yes, sir. I want you to talk to my partner,

Detective Scott Michaels, while I check your daughter's room."

Roger led Ben out of the room and down the hall. The house was all one floor, laid out in a big U-shape around a pool in the back. A place of barely beige and white, chrome and glass. Cold. Nothing could feel at home here but ghosts.

Ben felt alien and abrupt in this place.

"You think the father is good for this?" Ben asked Roger.

"Nope. I think you got an Amber." He opened the door to the room of a young female. But no boy-band posters on the walls, no heaps of this and piles of that. Clean, orderly, the room of someone who knew where things were. Thick, barely beige carpet, snowy bed linens, cream walls, white crown molding, a plasma TV on the wall across from the bed, a laptop computer on the cleared desk. A clock and lamp on the night table. Ben snapped on his gloves and opened the drawer. An iPod and an Emily Dickinson anthology.

Ben opened the book. "She wrote in this book. In ink. I wouldn't expect that." His brow furrowed.

"There's a bunch of stuff about fathers here. Maybe she has some issues with her own?" He slid the book into an evidence bag.

Roger interrupted. "Bed slept in. Room clean. Look at the glass."

Ben leaned over. "Window punched through from outside. Look at that." He squatted and peered at the carpet. "Damn."

"That's what I thought," Roger said.

"You check the father?"

"Haven't looked at his shoes. But eyeballing his feet, I'd say he's not even close."

Ben stood up. "Get a picture of that print and the girl's stats. Crime Scene needs to be here ten minutes ago. We've got a kidnapping by an unsub and time is against us."

Ben shook his head. "An Amber. Scott will wet his pants."

KYLE

"I'm not going to lie. I enjoyed it. I did. Cass sent my brother off that limb and she had to pay."

"See, that confuses me," the big cop said. "If that's the truth, why didn't you just tie her up in the greenhouse?"

"She had to end up just like David," I said.

"Then why didn't you hang her? Pin notes to her?"

A shudder rippled across my shoulders. This guy must be sick.

CASS

"Is that all you got?"

The voice came from my right hand. I shrieked. Where was he? My hand smacked the top of the box. He wasn't in here. He could hear me? Could he see me?

"What are you doing down there? So quiet?" His voice was low and smug. Whispering.

Panic surged through me. The bad dream. Someone in my ear. The hard arms pinning me. The sting in my arm followed by a hot arc into my muscle and a warm flush spreading across my chest that took me back down into sleep.

Adrenaline had cleared my head now. That voice had broken the window. He had probably drugged me. Yes, that quick hot pain and that cool voice. And then he had taken me.

Who?

Why?

Where?

What did he mean "down there"?

My head spun and my chest burned as I consciously tried to gulp air. There was air. I could breathe but I wanted more. In a dark box, feeling like weights pressed against me, rolled me flat, squeezed out the air. I sucked it in, proving I could. Demonstrative evidence that I was alive.

What did he mean "down there"?

I sobbed. But I didn't scream anymore. My throat was raw and I knew that voice wanted the screaming. And if he wanted it, it wouldn't do me any good. Not if I made it easy.

I had to wipe my nose and mouth with my left hand before I strangled on my own snot and tears.

Gasping and gulping in the damned blind dark.

Flat on my back with a psycho whispering in my ear.

"Cass? You're too quiet. I can hear you scream,

but I can't hear you cry. You are, aren't you? Sure you are."

I clamped my eyes down hard and grit my teeth.

He knows my name.

He didn't grab a stranger.

He grabbed *me.*

Someone I know put me in a box, in the dark, and he wants me to scream. He wants me terrified.

And I am.

But I won't scream. Not if he wants me to.

I held my breath, went rigid with the effort of listening.

And I heard it.

Footsteps. Vibrations. Above me.

My head lolled back. The footsteps were muffled like there was padding, lots of thick padding between the monster and me.

Dirt?

That smell like a new garden.

Earth?

My muscles went loose.

Not relaxed . . .

Hopeless.

New panic. Dragging the deep, hard breaths, trying to store all the oxygen I could.

Down there.

The smell of soil that's been turned for a new garden.

The chill.

Down there.

Muffled footsteps above me.

The size and shape of this box.

The total dark.

I had been buried alive.

Buried.

Alive.

Buried.

BEN

"Mr. McBride, what size shoe do you wear?"

Ted looked at Ben like he'd just grown an extra head. "Shoe size? You're going to find my daughter armed with my *shoe size*?"

"Nine, nine and a half?"

"Nine. Do we make jokes about my small feet now?"

"There's a shoe print on the carpet by the window in your daughter's bedroom and it's an eleven, by my eye."

Ted's mouth fell open. He shut it slowly. "Oh my god. Someone took my girl from my own house while I was asleep. This house is wired with every kind of alarm . . ." He looked away. "I get careless. I watch television, toss back a few drinks, don't remember to set the alarms. It's such a safe neighborhood, you know, the best people, the —"

Ben sat in a chair and pulled it close. "We need a recent picture. Names of friends. Addresses. Tell me about her mother. Where is she? Would she take your daughter?"

Ted took a deep breath and straightened up. "I'll get the pictures. There's a million of them. She's practically on every page of the yearbook." He took a step, then stopped, faced Ben, and established eye contact. "And I'll tell you something about my daughter, Detective. I don't know who took her, but unless he . . ." Ted shielded his eyes with his hand. He cleared his throat. "Cass will find a way to come home." Ted removed his hand and regained his composure. He straightened his back and again locked eyes with Ben. "Cass knows how to take care of herself. I taught her that."

KYLE

"Why did I bury her?"

I sat back in the chair. "Because it's what the Kirbys do. We bury things. We shove them out of sight. I didn't want to look at her, but I did want to torture her. So I grabbed her, dumped dirt over her, but made sure she understood why she was there. Tortured her the same way she had tortured David."

"But she didn't bury David." This was from the big cop.

"I don't get how she tortured your brother. You want to explain that for us?"

Big cop with the statements; little cop with the questions. My head hurt and I put my forehead down on the table. "It's complicated."

I was so quiet I could hear the cops breathing. Finally the baby cop cleared his throat. His signal for me to start talking again.

I turned my face without lifting my head. "I said I wanted to tell this my way. Maybe David went off that limb alone, but it wasn't suicide. It was murder. And someone has to pay for that. And that's not going to happen unless I tell it right. And you're hammering at me with questions and yammering at me to get things in the order you want. Shit, you're just like her."

I rocked my face to the other side, seeking the cool surface against my skin. "Now, I want something cold to drink, and some aspirin. And get that camera out of my face. I'll talk later if you step off and leave me alone for a while."

I couldn't make eye contact with the big cop.

"I can't get my mind right. You guys are screwing with my head. Can you leave me alone in here? And turn off the lights?"

CASS

Oh god, this was real.

"You've figured it out, huh, Cass?"

His voice snapped me back and I could feel him pace back and forth across my . . . grave.

"This not-talking shit is just pissing me off, Cass. You don't want to do that."

More pacing.

I cried, but no sobs. Quiet tears.

"Push in the button that's under your thumb and talk, Cass. I'm warning you. You won't like what happens if you don't."

His voice was slow and measured. Serious as — well, death. But I didn't answer. I couldn't.

And what did he expect me to say?

A spot of light as big as a silver dollar appeared

above my face (*not blind!*), then the light blotted out and something showered down on me. Dirt. In my nostrils and mouth. The light appeared again for an instant then disappeared.

I turned my head, spit, and cleared my nose and mouth, fear causing me to jerk up and bang my head, knees, and shoulders into the top and side of the box. I hit the button.

"Stop, please, don't do that again. Please."

"There now. Got you talking. That's what I want."

What did he want me to say?

"Cass?"

"Yes, don't throw dirt on me, please. I . . . don't understand what's going on." A sob escaped. I couldn't help it. My fingers again scrabbled the rough wood above me, ripping what was left of the skin and nails. I pounded the tape-bound hand, then pulled it closer to my face and pushed in the square button. "Please, let me go. I don't know who you are so I can't tell anybody anything. Just let me go. Let me out of here."

I was begging him. I knew it would get me

nowhere. I watch TV. I read *those* kinds of books. The bad guy likes the begging. . . . He gets off on it.

But what else did I have? I WAS BURIED IN A BOX!

"Please. Just let me go. I won't tell anyone."

"Oh, I know you won't tell anyone. I'm so sure you won't that I don't care if you know who I am."

I bit down on my lip until I tasted blood. He was going to kill me.

He paced again. Across my chest. Back across my head. He stopped.

"My name is Kyle Kirby. David Kirby is — *was* my little brother."

I didn't know until that moment that a person's teeth could actually chatter. But mine did. Fear, real fear is physical. David's name was a cold wave that washed over me, and I shivered from toenails to teeth. I shook too hard to keep my left fist clenched; my teeth wouldn't grit; nothing worked according to my will.

"Having a guilty little moment in there?" His whisper was calm and quiet. "Wondering how much I know? How much to deny?"

Teeth still clattering, I couldn't have answered if I had anything to say.

The first time I saw Kyle he was half naked. Buff and blond and hot in the icy Aryan way. Sweat glazed his tan, muscled torso and he attacked the weeds in the country club flower beds as if he hated each one.

"Hottie alert," Erica said. "Kyle Kirby. My mom knows his dad." She started ticking off stats like a reporter. "He's on the baseball team. Moody. Doesn't date much. Never had a steady girlfriend, as far as I know. In fact, I don't know much more. Keeps to himself."

Erica's mom had dropped us at the club for an afternoon at the pool. Three girls from school, juniors, sashayed in front of us.

"Hey, Kyle," one of them singsonged. He glanced over, wiping sweat off his cheek by hunching one shoulder and shoving his face across it. He never removed his grip on the weeds. He didn't speak but gave a half-assed nod and jerked up the weeds in the same motion.

Standoffish catnip, I thought. He never glanced at Erica or me. And that was the surest way to my heart.

When school started, I made it my business to find out his schedule. Following Ted's rules, I knew to do my research, then I managed to be "around" or "just leaving" the area where Kyle would be. It was a first for me to pursue a boy. The only reaction I got for my trouble was one guarded look. Something akin to distaste. When a deal goes sour, accept and stop selling. I forgot about Kyle Kirby.

The spot of light appeared above me.

"See this, Cass? That's the end of an air tube." A snap and the light dimmed. "I put a filter on it — keeps out dirt and stuff. Now I let the tube fall along the ground." Darkness again. "And you can't see the light from my flashlight. In faaaact" — he stretched this out like he was singing it — "you should be seeing pretty much what David sees."

A groan escaped me.

"Feeling sorry for yourself? Hoping you weren't buried?" He laughed, low and seemingly satisfied. "Well, believe it. You're not in a nice casket like David. You don't deserve satin lining and pillows. You just get a crate for your grave.

"But, I wasn't sure you'd know *why* you were there. I couldn't just leave you. Honestly, Cass, you're too damn self-centered to figure it out without me to pound it into your head."

Self-centered? He buried me because I was *self-centered*? Not even I could think this was all about me. This had to be about the note — about words that I didn't expect David to see. But, let's get real here, there had to be a lot wrong with David to go sailing off a limb because a girl rejected him. And since when does self-centered stack up against kidnapping and burying someone alive? Think about that awhile, asswipe.

"So you have an air tube and there's a pump to get all your carbon dioxide out through a little hole in the other end. It's crude, but it will work for a while. I don't have a lot of time anyway."

"What do you mean? A lot of time? For what?"

He paused and paced above me. "I don't know how long you've got either."

"How long for what? What are you talking about?" I screamed.

"Damn, you took a long time to wake up. I wondered if I'd killed you with that drug. I hope you drank a lot of water before you went to bed on Friday. Dehydration is —"

"Kyle —"

"Don't! Do *not* say my name. You have no right to use it. Say my name and dirt comes down the tube. Got that?"

I nodded.

"Answer!"

"Yes. I've got it. I won't use your name. I won't."

"And there's something else. Try to deny, just try to deny that you did this to David, make excuses for yourself, and I jerk the air tube and walk away. Understand?"

I almost nodded again but then realized he couldn't see me.

"Understood."

"Fine, now it's late and I have to go back to . . . a whole different kind of hell. You stay here and I'll be back. Or maybe not."

And nothing. Not even vibrations.

I was alone.

BEN

Ted pulled a picture from a leather frame angled precisely on a polished chrome desktop that seemed to float on glass or Lucite legs. It gave Ben the jeebies. How could you put your feet up on a desk like that? Drop a heavy box on it? Nothing in this house felt like it had substance. Except Ted. Maybe that was the point.

"Cass knows where she's going and how to get there," Ted said as he handed the picture over. "She's going East to school, PR and marketing. She's going to be an events manager. Handle the movers and shakers. She knows how to do that. Network. I taught her to read people. She's a natural."

Ben looked at the photograph. Attractive, but not threateningly so. Poised. Leaning against a large tree. Dressed in white shorts, peach knit shirt, athletic shoes, and socks. She gripped a tennis racquet loosely in a tanned hand. Brown hair pulled back, makeup natural, smile easy and confident. Wholesome, Ben thought. An old-fashioned word, but that's how she appeared.

A quick search of her clothes didn't show a split personality. The kid didn't pose as an angel then go hoochie mamma to parties.

Ted paced the carpet. "Who would kidnap Cass?" He tugged his rumpled hair. "My ex doesn't have the nerve. Even if she doped Cass and took her, when Cass woke up, she'd just leave. Leatha knows that." Ted turned and paced back the other direction. "Cass can visit anytime and she doesn't want to. No, Leatha's not a possibility." He stopped and looked at Ben. "Do you think I should call her?"

"If you don't mind, if you haven't told her, we'd like to do that," Ben said. "It helps to see someone when we tell them about a kidnapping if there's any chance –"

"I get it," Ted said. He resumed pacing. "Sure. But I'm telling you. Waste of time."

Ben nodded. "Probably, but talking about a waste of time . . . you mind taking a polygraph? Personally, I don't take you for a suspect."

Ted waved him off. "Fine. But I could talk my way past your electrodes even if I was guilty. Cass could too. We have a way."

KYLE

The dark soothed me a little, but the quiet — nobody can understand how great quiet sounds unless he's never had it. Or what it feels like to talk *with* a person when you usually have someone talk *at* you. At you. And at you.

"Do you have flying dreams?" David asked.

"I think most people have them. But yeah, I do."

We were in the park. I sat on the bench reading A Confederacy of Dunces. "Can't you sit like a normal person?"

"I'm not normal. Not even close. Ask her." David's feet were on the back of the bench and his head hung over the seat. "Besides, I like watching things upside down."

"Knock yourself out, bro."

"I know why we have flying dreams."

I sighed and closed my book. I might be here for the quiet, but David had so few opportunities for conversation. "Tell me."

"Nope."

"Arrggh." Sometimes he was a cretin.

David put on a fake Freud voice. As if he knew anything about Freud. "The answer is here. Right here in this park. You just have to look." He dropped the accent. "And you'll know why my *flying* dreams are always bad."

I looked around. Kids playing with each other. Mothers watching. Dogs playing with the bigger kids or adults. Little kids in sandboxes.

"I don't . . ." And then I saw what he meant. A little kid flew. Just flew right into the air.

The kid in the sandbox had been playing with a pail and shovel, filling up the pail and dumping it out, filling his shoes with sand as he dumped. Then he filled the pail and held it high and dumped the sand over his head.

She swooped down like a vulture. One arm under his butt and the other around his chest.

"Stop that this minute. If you can't play nice, you can't play."

And then he was airborne. One minute his sneakers rooted in sand, the next he's picked straight up and flying away, his feet dangling over the grass and zipping along through the air with no control, the wind against his face until he landed astraddle her hip, her voice in his ear in the punishment zone.

Sure, I knew why David's flying dreams were nightmares. And I knew how that voice wasn't just in his dreams. It followed him everywhere.

The door opened and the light flared.

The big cop stood, placed his knuckles on the table, and leaned, straight-armed, toward me. His tone was gentle. Kind. And leading. "Kyle, I think you need to help yourself here. Hope that girl makes it and keep talking."

CASS

He was gone. Somehow I was certain that he wasn't faking. Wasn't a few feet away, listening. Getting off on my screams.

And I did scream. Ripping my throat raw. First they were words. *Help me.* Then just *help.* Then just ragged sounds in all sizes and kinds. They were angry, terrified, primal, and the last, the worst, lost.

I thrashed, kicked, hammered, and battered. My skin split and bruised and I broke a finger. The pain was good. It drove the fear off to the side a little. When one corner of the box edged a fraction of an inch out as a result of one mulish kick, I froze.

The box was prison and protection. It kept the

earth from crushing and suffocating me. Fighting my coffin would kill me quicker than accepting it.

Okay, I told myself. Stop. Cass. Stop and think. Try to go Zen. Take a deep breath. I stilled myself then drew in a breath, soft and even, held it, then let it out slow. Did it again. Again.

That's better. Now. Don't think about where you are. You're in the dark. A dark room, resting. Your eyes are closed and you're resting. Come on, Cass, you can do this. Concentrate.

Think. Slow. Breathe. In. Out. Slow.

I imagined myself stretched out in a field of grass, at night, stars overhead, my eyes closed.

Breathe slow. In. Out. Slow. Slow.

Good. Calming down. Good.

Now, think.

Concentrate.

Fear is a weapon.

His weapon.

Right now, you're shooting yourself with his gun.

Accept the fear and deal with it. Just fuckin' deal.

Breathe.

Slow.

In and out.

Work through this.

Let me think like my dad.

Kyle Kirby.

Kyle Kirby put me in this box and covered me up with dirt and now he says I can't say his name.

It's all about control. Kyle has physical control. I have to get mental control. That starts with me. I have to get control.

Kyle.

Kyle.

Kyle Kirby.

There. It's mine.

I'll think your name all I want, jackass. I control what's in my head.

But then panic swooped back over me and I dragged in harsh, rapid breaths. Why did the dark seem so heavy?

Breathe.

Slow.

In and out.

Don't think about where you are.

Get the *where* out of your head. Concentrate on *why* you're here.

Answer: David Kirby.

I closed my eyes and tears leaked out.

David Kirby.

Dorky David Kirby asked me out. What made him think he could dare ask me? Can U imagine? How far down the food chain would he have to go for a date? God, I thought he was gay.

If our school gestapo allowed cell phones, we could text and none of this would have happened. But I scrawled it on a piece of notebook paper and folded the page in half once and then again, and then over on itself. I left it under the seat of my desk in American History.

Erica would be in the class the next hour. She was coming from across campus and I had to scoot in the other direction, so I couldn't hang around for a handoff. This had been our mail system since September, when we had to reinstate our sixth grade CIA, dead-drop, secret agent stuff that we had made up back when we had yearned to be spies.

David Kirby had shuffled up to me before class, tugging one ear and clearing his throat. "Um, Cass, I wanted to ask you something."

I would have swept right past him, but I was stunned. David Kirby. Loser with a capital *L*. Well, capitalize *all* the letters. Had he spoken to me?

It wasn't like he was an upright maggot. Not ugly, but not good-looking by any means. Face too long, expression to match. Spaniel eyes. Not cute, needy. A guy you want to push away. He was skinny, always in clothes a size too big, looking like his bones had been pitched into his shirts and pants unassembled. Long-sleeved shirts, buttoned up to the chin. Good clothes — Hilfiger, Lauren, Abercrombie & Fitch — but it was the way he wore them. He leached the cool factor out of them.

David Kirby was one of those kids that gets shoved in their lockers, gets their butt cheeks taped together in gym, well, if he gets any attention at all. Never saw him with a girl. Ever. Just skulking around alone. Not banger, not Goth, not goat roper, born-again, grade-point grubber, or jock-remora. Not even one of those who floats between the groups. David Kirby couldn't be described in positives — just what he wasn't. He wasn't a wannabe. He wasn't-ever-*gonna*-be.

And he had stepped into my zone.

I turned to him, he made eye contact, and I looked around, making sure he got the idea that I was embarrassed to be seen talking to him.

"I wondered," he sputtered. "I mean, I'd like it if you'd . . ." He tugged his ear again. God, soon his lobes would be different lengths. "If you'd go out with me. This weekend. Or next, maybe. Whenever you're free, to a movie or whatever. Miniature golf."

He said it in *one* breath. Eyes on the floor. Had he rehearsed? I didn't know whether to laugh or gag. Either made *me* look bad.

"I know miniature golf sounds lame," David continued. "But at a movie you just sit, and the golf thing, it's so lame that it can be fun, and you get a chance to talk, get to know each other. But, you have to promise to let me cheat, 'cause I'm lousy."

From someone else . . . it might have been almost, well, cute. But honestly, David Kirby? I think not. Now I was doing the throat clearing. "David, that's, like, really sweet, you know? But, I'm pretty tied up for a while. I'll have to get back to you."

I remembered to flash him my totally famous Cass McBride dimpled grin/head tilt. It was October, a week until Homecoming, and those ballots were already cast. I would be the first junior Homecoming Queen ever.

But being the first junior Prom Queen this coming spring was going to be a lot harder and I had to keep the charm thing going. Every vote counted.

I twinked away as David was narfing something about, "Thanks, I'll wait to hear from you."

The bell rang and we all sat, slouched or sprawled, in our desks. Our teacher's a coach. Translation: We read a chapter, answer the questions at the end, and have a test on Fridays. If the chapter is short, Coach shows a movie while we nap. Today we read and copied answers from each other while Coach drew basketball plays. And I swear David made calf eyes at me the whole class. I wrote the note to Erica and stashed it in the desk.

After the escape-bell rang, I sailed up the aisle but noticed David moving at the back of the room toward my desk. I stopped. Shit, he must have watched me squirrel the note away.

"Forgot something," I said as I tried to push my way against the toward-the-door tramplers. Then I saw David slide the note into his pocket.

One Prom Queen vote lost for damn sure, I thought.

I never thought that a few careless words scrawled on a piece of paper could put two people in graves.

BEN

Ben stood on the porch with his partner and Officers Ford and Oakley. "Roger and Tyrell, you are assigned to my detail. Tyrell, I want you to protect the scene. Keep McBride under your thumb until Crime Scene gets here. He can call his lawyer and that's it. I'm sending the polygraph guy here unless somebody squawks.

"Phone crew will set up for a ransom call. They'll take over the babysitting and you can join Roger."

He turned to Roger. "You head to the station, later Ford will join you. I'll get a couple of other officers on it. You'll be in charge of the group. Do interviews. Concentrate on the school. Friends, teachers, counselors.

"It's Saturday — that's going to slow it down. Call the principal and counselors first and arrange for the kids to come to the school for the interviews. Make 'em more comfortable. Interview close friends, boyfriends, names you get from the father, at their homes, talk to their parents too. Bring her best girlfriend and current boyfriend to the station. If anybody finds a diary, a journal, a what-do-you-call-'em —" He snapped his fingers at Scott then turned his palm up in question.

"Blog," Scott answered. "On her computer. A Web site."

"Right, one of those. Get the techs on her computer. Anybody finds something like that — I want to know yesterday."

Ben checked his watch. Frowned.

"I'll get Adam checking phone records and the father's finances. Scott, use that snazzy little cell phone and get us on a flight to Louisiana. You've got your first Amber and we're at least twelve hours into the first forty-eight."

KYLE

"You guys gonna let me tell the story the way I need to tell it now?"

The big cop sat down across from me. He didn't say anything, but he led me with his silence. The puppy cop leaned in the corner with his arms crossed over his chest. Oooooh. Bad cop. Fine by me. My headache was a little better. I relaxed into the chair. I was here to talk.

"I don't think Cass McBride was aware I existed until I told her my name. But I knew her.

"It was August. The heat was brutal even with the school's central air blowing full tilt. Just about everybody was in the usual first-day dress code: baggy shorts, tees, flip-flops. Looking like we crawled out of bed and were ready for the beach. And then I saw her."

I elbowed Chris Monahan. "Who the hell is that?"

Chris grinned and made a cross out of his index fingers like he was warding off a vampire. "Cass McBride. New freshman, but you don't have a chance. You're on the baseball team, but you're not captain of the baseball team. Out of your league. She's so far out of your league, she's even out of mine."

I don't know how a freshman walked that razor edge. Confidence without arrogance. Just one look at her and I knew there was nothing but internal calm and quiet. There must be quiet in her home. Peace all the time. She wore it on her like a personal air-conditioning system.

No sheen of sweat above her lip. And no beach casual for Cass McBride. She wore a white skirt. Short enough to show a lot of tanned leg, but long enough to force imagination into play. It moved with her, swung, flirty-like, and her tee was silky, with a vest on top. All white. Layers of clothes and she was fresh and unrumpled.

All those layers of cool. Down so deep. My cool had a

shallow root system. I wanted what she had. If I couldn't
have it . . . why should she?

"Maybe this can explain Cass McBride," I said. "That first day, she carried a bright pink purse and she had buckled her watch to the strap. By noon, I'll bet fifty girls — not just wannabes, but some of the Senior-Rule-the-School girls — had their watches buckled to the straps of their purses. By the next day, it was an epidemic."

The cop was tapping the table, drumming with his fingers. "I know it sounds like I picked her out, but I didn't. David did that himself. I guess I'm trying to show you why he would."

And why hadn't I known David would pick Cass? Could I have stopped it right there?

CASS

I didn't even tell Erica about the note. She's weird about stuff like that. If I told Erica, she would get that look. Her oh-you-can't-take-the-kitty-to-the-pound look.

She asked me once why, if I was Miss Everything, did I have to be so mean sometimes?

Because, Erica, if you're sitting still, the others are catching up. That's why. You have to keep the force field operating. Keep the other guys short and you'll always be tall. Whatever.

So why out myself to Erica? I doubted David had many friends, so he wouldn't tell anyone. No harm, no foul.

Until the next day.

"Cass, did you hear?"

"Hear what?"

"David Kirby? Do you know him?"

I got interested in the contents of my locker. "David Kirby?" I waited for what else Erica would say. Had he called her? Taken out an ad? Read my note over the radio?

She eased up close. "He killed himself," she whispered.

My heart didn't skip a beat. It skipped then stalled. My breath did too.

"What?"

"I know, it's horrible. My mom got the call early."

Erica's mother is a medical examiner, which moved this from rumor to reality.

"Cass, he hung himself. From a big tree on his front lawn. He pinned a note on his body. Not on his shirt. On his body." She whispered the last part as if it were shameful.

I licked my lips. They were dry, but my mouth suddenly filled with saliva, signaling that I needed to pray to the porcelain goddess. Now.

I dropped my books and dashed for the bathroom. I didn't make it to a stall but I at least caught the sink. Scattering Becka, Meg, and Leslie as they lipsticked and mascaraed.

"EWWWWW!"

"Gross!"

"Cass, that's an eight-hundred dollar purse!"

I retched again, and then ran water into the mess and moved to another sink to wash my face.

"Sorry, sorry." I flapped my hands. "Tell me I missed your purse, Becka."

Becka inspected her turquoise leather trophy. "Looks like I grabbed it just in time."

"Thank god," I said. I grabbed a wad of towels and mopped my mouth. "I'd hate to have to pay you for that thing."

"Knocked up or hung over?" This from a nobody in heavy eye makeup and baseball-sized earrings. She leaned against a stall and smoked a home-rolled. I ignored her.

Erica appeared at my elbow, toting my books. "Cass, are you okay?"

"Stomach's been wonky," I said. "And hearing that shit about a note pinned to . . ." I stopped and shut my eyes. "I got a visual, you know?"

I braced both hands on the counter and hung my head. "I think that Kirby guy is, well, was in my history class."

The bathroom went stone silent.

"Was?" Becka asked. "What do you mean?"

And the place went beehive. Voices buzzed in a knot. Questions and answers fell all over each other. I gave Erica a nod and we edged out.

"He was in your history class?"

"Yeah, I'm pretty sure. He's one of those you never notice, though."

Erica nodded. "His brother graduated two years ago. Cute."

"Kyle Kirby is David Kirby's brother?"

Erica nodded. "Hard to believe, isn't it? Nothing alike."

I wondered what kind of parents could have produced two such different sons.

The answer to that question could kill me now.

BEN

"This place is seriously in the swamp," Scott said.

Ben strode along the plank walk to the café/coffeehouse/boat rental/bait shop where Leatha McBride worked for her brother-in-law.

"Do you think there's alligators in that water?"

"I would expect so. And water moccasins and a few other things that can kill you."

"I can understand why the kid didn't want to come here," Scott said.

"Looks like bait and boats are in the bottom part," Ben said as they arrived at the building. It was on stilts, the bottom screened in. An outside flight of stairs led to the top story. The smell of coffee and spices wafted out.

Ben and Scott entered the big room, with a

scraped wooden floor, and a scattering of tables covered with red-checked oilcloths. Ben produced his badge to the woman that approached.

"I'm Detective Ben Gray and this is Detective Scott Michaels. We'd like to talk to Leatha McBride." Ben knew he was talking to Cass's mother already. Ted McBride may have boasted that his DNA ruled his daughter's character, but clearly it was Leatha McBride who supplied the girl's looks. She studied Ben's shield and made eye contact with him, glanced at Scott, then gestured to a quiet corner in the little café.

"You don't look surprised to see a detective from Texas," Ben said.

"I'm assuming Ted is making a demand of some sort," she said. Ben thought she sounded tired and sad, but not angry. Resigned, maybe. Certainly not antsy.

"I can't imagine what it would be," she continued.

"Your daughter is missing," Ben said. "Kidnapped, we think."

He watched the shock register. But the woman

sat mute, her only movement a slight shake in the hand that strayed to her mouth.

"When?"

"Last night."

"Tell me."

Ben knew from her urgent whisper what this mother wanted.

"No blood at the scene. No reason to think there's been violence to your daughter. Still in the first forty-eight hours. That's good, but we don't have a suspect and time's doing what time does."

"You flew here. You think I'm involved."

"Noncustodial parent — always first interview. Forensics has work to do and officers are doing local interviews."

"I didn't take her or ask anyone else to do it."

Ben listened.

"There's no reason." Leatha's hands were trembling. "You haven't met her, but believe me, this is no place Cass would stay." She spread her fingers on the table, pressing them against the checked cloth and staring down at them. Nails trimmed short. Unpolished.

"Would Ted do this?" Ben asked.

"Is Ted capable of kidnapping his own child for financial gain? Is he that callous?" Leatha looked away. "Certainly. But, you have to understand what Cass represents to Ted and you'd know it's impossible."

"Tell me more," Ben said.

She got up and walked to the back of the café, returning with three mugs of coffee. "I recommend using cream even if that's not your habit. This is laced with chicory. The Cajun way." Leatha kept her eyes averted and appeared to be fighting for composure as she poured cream into her mug until the dark coffee turned the color of caramel. She spooned in sugar. Four teaspoons. Ben sipped and wondered briefly if the brew could peel paint.

After her coffee ceremony, Leatha seemed to have her thoughts organized and herself in control. She sipped, set her mug down.

"What do you need to know?"

"Start with Ted. He inherit his money?"

"Ted came from nothing. Dirt-poor. What people call trailer trash. Didn't even finish high school.

But he scratched and clawed and made money. He sold insurance and vacuum cleaners. And then moved up to copiers. He's sold everything."

"Where did you come into the picture?"

"He met me along the way. During the insurance phase. I was so right for him then. I was pretty and compliant." She sipped. "And he took my breath away. He set his sights on me and he was going to win me no matter what. That was heady stuff for a young girl."

She noted Ben's flinch when he tasted the coffee. Smiling, but without a word, she took Ben's cup and Scott's cup, left the table, and returned with refilled cups. "Sissy coffee. No chicory."

"Where was this?" Ben asked.

"Lake Charles. Then he got a shot at selling copiers in New Orleans. Big company, big opportunities for growth. We moved. Whenever Ted made enough money in one place, he wanted to move on. Change jobs and reinvent himself."

"How did that work out for Ted?"

"He made a big pile of money and wanted to move on. This time it was Houston real estate. And he told people that he graduated from LSU and that I had done local modeling. We had Cass. We were the perfect little family. He paid a woman for a crash course in manners. The right fork, the proper introductions, the way to dress. Ted didn't just want to be rich — he wanted the appearance of refinement."

Leatha's smile was crooked. "He had to buy lessons in understating his wealth. But he was still hired help.

"We moved again. Ted opened his own business. We lived in one of the best sections of one of the most exclusive subdivisions. But not the areas where the houses only go from one family member to the next. Ted wants *that* kind of class."

"Okay, that's Ted and money. Tell me about Ted and you. Ted and Cass."

Leatha seemed to think a minute. "The thing with Ted is you have to keep proving yourself to him. Like he keeps proving himself to the world. And I wasn't pretty anymore. Wasn't witty. So, I wasn't any help to him. Now Cass is the way he can get what he wants. Ted *needs* her to marry someone with a pedigree. And he wouldn't sully that with a kidnapping."

Leatha was through with her coffee. She folded her hands. "Do I sound like a prepared speech? A recitation? It is, really. You have to understand that I've spent years going through this, looking at every little detail over and again. Discussing it with my sister until I wore her patience thin. I have dozens of notebooks filled with my thoughts."

She sighed. "The only way I can resign myself to the thought that my daughter cares little to nothing for me is to divorce myself emotionally from it."

Ben nodded. "That's something police know a lot about."

"Sad, isn't it?" Leatha said.

Ben drank his sissy coffee as Leatha explained her own decision to leave. "She wasn't my daughter anymore. Not in any way that counted. It's not that Cass is heartless. It's that she's never heard her heart. Not yet. She lives in her head. She calculates, figuring the bottom line, just like Ted. And I no longer had a place in her column of credits."

Sadness overtook her then. "Excuse me, please." She left the room, heading for the back. Ben imagined the kitchen and bathroom were through the swinging door that Leatha pushed through. He and Scott waited without speaking.

When Leatha returned, her voice shook, but she seemed to know what she wanted to say.

She looked at Ben. Caught his eye and held it. "She and Ted . . . I don't think they love each other either, not real love, like a daughter and father — it's pretense. For him she's like one of the expensive cars at his dealership — beautiful and shiny, where he can see his reflection."

"What does Cass get from it?"

Leatha shrugged. "Cass needs to prove herself too. You know, to Ted. It's the only way he'll love her . . . and . . . she loves the lights of the showroom floor."

Her eyes went bright with tears. "Find her, please. Bring her home, even if it's not to me. I need her home and safe."

KYLE

"You're dickin' us around. What's a watch on a pink purse got to do with anything? Are you going to quit the crap and tell us what happened?" The young cop shot out of the corner and slammed a palm down on the table in front of my face.

Like someone screaming at me was new. "We're getting there," I said.

The young cop looked pissed. Too bad. The big cop looked like he might not trust me. If he'd keep listening, he'd catch up. Or if he didn't, I didn't much care.

"David was like my dad. A doormat. But I think my dad gave up on wanting her to love him. Or got enough of it. I don't know if it makes any difference. But he let her walk all over him."

I looked at the young cop, who was back in his

corner. "Is he out there? My dad? You called him, right? Did he even come back?"

The big cop answered. Wanting to keep control in his hands probably. "He's here. Looks like a truck wreck. I don't think he understands. Hell, I still don't understand."

I started jiggling my leg and looking around the room. Suddenly anxious and jittery. "I know this is off the wall, but it's been bugging me. Do you know if Cass's name is actually Cassandra? I mean, wouldn't that be the final touch of irony? Cassandra was the prophetess of doom."

CASS

How many hours in this box?

Kyle said Friday. He said he hoped I drank a lot of water on Friday. That means it's not Friday now. It's at least Saturday. I went to bed late, so I don't think this is early morning. He said I took a long time to wake up, long enough that he thought maybe he'd killed me. God knows I'm stiff. And godawful thirsty.

Who knew lying down could hurt so much? My joints ached, and my back. I moved every part of me that I could, but hit wood each time. I found myself working my jaw because I clenched it so hard, hunching one shoulder, then the other; any kind of movement was relief. What did this stiffness mean?

I was shivering again. From fear? Or was I chilled from being underground for so long?

Panic brought my heartbeat to a rapid staccato. I was hyperaware of how dry my mouth was and how I dragged in stale air.

I needed to change the subject.

Cass McBride will not be helpless. She makes things happen.

She wins.

Time to forget where I am.

Put it away.

Plan.

Focus.

Start the campaign.

I learned a lot of things in school, but in the leather pub chair of my father's office I got my real education.

Dad almost always had dinner out. Either with clients or working late at his office. I'd eat alone but wait for him to come home. He'd head straight to his study for his bottle of Dickel and a glass. I'd come in when I knew he'd settled into his chair and loosened his tie. If I were any more like a Labrador retriever, I'd have his slippers in my mouth.

He'd tip his glass to me in acknowledgment. Dad never got drunk, but his boozy breath and relaxed attitude meant it was time for him to reveal the secrets of Ted's world. The world of salesman-ship and negotiating the deal.

In one important lesson, Ted nailed me with his steel-blue stare. "You research your customer as much as your product." He put down the glass. "Tell me why."

"You can't sell the product until you match it to the customer's need?"

Ted nodded, pleased, then slapped the table, startling me. "Never make it a question. Answer with authority. If you speak with authority, people listen. Walk with confidence. Keep your eyes straight ahead but watch the people around you, using your peripheral vision. Don't get caught off guard. It matters, Cass. It always matters."

Sometimes we played chess and he instructed me about his world as he moved his frosted glass pieces around the board.

"It's called a sales campaign for a good reason. It's warfare of a kind. You capture the sale. The battleground is your mind, and your weapons are words."

I never beat him at chess. I put him in check once with my clear glass queen. I couldn't interpret his smile. Then in one move he eluded capture and in two more had me in checkmate. "Don't sell your opponent short, Cass. In the art of the deal, you play until it's over. And you don't ever let an opponent stand back up.

73

Don't let him have the chance to take what you've gained." He knocked my king over with his, and then put his king safely back in the padded box.

I don't know that I ever completely trusted Dad again. And I think that's what he wanted me to learn.

Once he leaned forward and gestured me close as if he was revealing the most important secret of all.

"You don't sell the product, Cass. You sell the customer his own self-doubt. You sell his shortcomings."

I guess he saw the doubt in my eyes, so he leaned further in and tapped the chrome desktop. "You have to figure out what he's missing in himself and you wrap that up in a bow and sell it to him."

He leaned back into his chair and sipped his drink. "Works like a charm."

As Dad gazed unblinkingly at the wall, I wondered briefly which of my self-doubts he had sold back to me. But I shoved that thought away. Then.

When I got older I got pissed that the only thing we talked about was Ted's World. But I still went and I kept listening. I knew what happened if Ted lost interest in you.

Dad swung open the glass doors of our new house, and I bounced inside.

"Mom, look. It's full of all new stuff. It's like living in heaven."

The house was white on white and cream. Glass and chrome. I felt wrapped in a cloud, floating through the halls and into my white-on-white room. The house wrapped around the only color, the glittering turquoise pool.

"Mom, aren't you coming in?"

I had raced through the house and Mom was still frozen in the doorway.

"Ted, you bought this without me? You bought all this furniture?"

"I had a decorator do it. We're not bringing a thing from the other house."

I squealed. "All new clothes!"

"Sure," Dad said. "Pastels and turquoise, cream and white — all to look good in the house."

Dad looked at Mom. "None of that awful brown you always wear, Leatha. It'd look like someone dropped a big turd on that couch."

I laughed at Dad's joke, but Mom didn't.

Mom stopped wearing brown and started wearing a lot of tan and she sort of disappeared. Faded into the walls of that house. Dad stalked through it. His steel-gray suits cutting through the clouds, my peaches and turquoises and pinks providing the color and warmth. Dad and I pulled into a unit and Mom floated alone. She just wasn't all that interesting.

But once she surprised me. That day she wasn't uninteresting at all.

Mom came into the kitchen. She put a suitcase next to the door and clutched a photo album. I recognized it. All my baby pictures. She wore a brownish loose top and tan pants. Shoes that nurses might wear. Where did she get those?

She sat, rested the album on the table but kept her fingers curled around the edge, as if one of us might grab it. Dad and I were eating scrambled eggs and toast that I made. He wore a suit with a royal-blue tie and I wore a turquoise silk blouse. Mom looked like a wren at a feeder with two jays.

"I have something to say," she said. "Do me the courtesy of not interrupting until I'm through."

A demand from Mom? This was new.

"Ted, I'm tired of agreeing with you. I have been stupid but that's changed."

Dad put his fork down and sat back in his chair. I could see he was stunned.

"Cass, I'm leaving and I'd like you to come with me. I doubt you will, but I'm begging you to leave."

"Where are you going?" I asked.

"Louisiana."

Mom was born there. Her sister taught school and her brother-in-law ran a bait shop/beer joint/crawfish boil place on the bayou.

Dad barked a laugh of disbelief. "What are you going to do for money? I'll hide my assets and you won't get a red cent."

"I'm going to waitress for Suzanne and Charlie."

"You're going to waitress?" I couldn't hide the shock. "Clean up other people's dirty plates? Take orders and get treated like dirt?"

"Why not? Mom said. "It's what I do here."

Ooookay. That set me back. Mom was dead-on and it didn't feel good. But like Dad, I had to assess my situation.

Mom loved me. I knew that. But she always would. If I left, Dad would wash his hands of me. To have Dad and Mom I had to stay with him. My friends were here. My life was here. And did I really want to trade a big house in a great neighborhood to go to the swamps and grow webs between my toes?

I'd take webs between my toes now. I'd take scales and a forked tongue. I'd sling crawfish and cut bait on the bayou rather than be here. Not much of a choice. Who's going to say, "Hey, sign me up for a box underground"?

Stop.

No box, ground, under.

My breath went ragged and I pulled it in and held it. Let it out. Slow.

Couldn't even let those words rent space in my head. I felt the adrenaline surge right through me. I was working for Zen. Calm, strong, and in control.

Back to Ted's Teachings.

Plan the Campaign.

First: What is my objective?

No-brainer. I want out of this box. Out from under this ground.

Okay.

Second: How do I achieve my objective?

I can't dig out. I don't know how far under I am. I'll suffocate.

I might wait until someone finds me.

What are the chances of that?

Sobs tightened my throat again.

Easy, Cass, breathe. In, out. In, slow, out, slow.

Great. Rescue — not an option.

So?

The only way out of here is through the guy that put me here. Like that's gonna happen.

Think a minute, though.

If Kyle wanted to kill me, I'd be dead. If he just wanted me to die knowing it was revenge for David, he could put a tape recording in here. There wouldn't be an air pump.

And he put in a walkie.

He wasn't done with me yet.

He wants something.

Something I have.

And if my dad taught me anything, it's that if someone wants something and someone else has it, there's a deal waiting to be made.

BEN

Ben entered the crime lab Saturday night. "Show me."

"What'da ya want first? What you don't have or what you do?"

"Get the bad news out of the way," Ben said.

The woman pulled a file from a pile on her desk. Red tab. Flipped it open, ran a French-tip manicured nail down a page.

"Nos on diary, journal, blog, e-mail, or phone text mail. Nothing in the IM's. Prints in the room match housekeeper, father, vic, best friend, and, what I find interesting for a teen girl, no one else. Nada. This kid doesn't let many people in her room."

She shrugged. "Or maybe they have an efficient housekeeper. Carpet. Love the carpet. Wool. Holds footprints like a glove. Print you saw is the best of six. But the great news about that one is that it's on the carpet but partially on the glass shards."

"Meaning . . . ?" Ben was smiling.

"Oh yeah, our bad guy is going to have some little cuts in the tread of his shoe. Maybe even glass particles."

Ben rubbed his hands together. "Any more?"

"From the depth of the print, he was carrying something heavy when he went out the window and stepped on the glass."

"He's not just heavy?"

"Partial print by a tree on the property. Possible match to the shoe print. Difference in depth that lets us know a little about weight. Definitely carrying something on the way out. I think your guy watched the house, left his print in the dirt around the tree in the dark. He was pretty careful. No other prints outside. No fingerprints inside. I'm running tests on the sheets to see if I can find presence of drugs. If he injected there could be a drop. Saturated cloth will leave some residue."

Ben opened his mouth to speak.

A French-tipped nail pointed him to silence. "Back to the nos. No hair. Must have worn a cap. Not finding transfer. Just some of the dirt from outside the vic's house. The sheets must have been fresh that day. Not even a lot of the kid's skin cells present. I think she was snatched soon after she went to sleep."

"Yup," Ben said. "Fits with the watching-at-the-tree theory. So we could have opportunistic crime. Somebody sees her, follows her home, and waits to grab her. Or we got somebody that knows the girl and knows where she lives and how to get there."

"Gated community?"

"Yeah, but a no-brainer to get by."

"I'll call when I get something on the drug tests."

"Why couldn't she keep a diary?" Ben said.

"I wish they all had talking dogs."

"You have a daughter, don't you?" Ben asked.

"She's sixteen. Knows the kid that was grabbed. She'll be sleeping in my room tonight."

KYLE

I looked at the big cop and then at the young one. "You guys got brothers?"

Big one nodded. Young one said, "Two sisters."

"Older or younger?" I asked the big cop.

"He's dead. Hit by a drunk driver when he was barely twenty. Killed his girlfriend at the same time. He was seven years older than me."

"Did you fight when you were kids?"

The big cop crossed his arms over his chest. "He probably got sick of me hanging around. I hero-worshipped him. He taught me to play basketball, baseball, kept me out of trouble."

"I was three years older than David and I used to get sick of him. I thought him being near me put me in her strike zone, you know? She'd be screaming at him, ragging on him about his grades or his clothes or how he looked, and he'd run into our room, where I was trying to keep out of the way. And she never ran out of steam, she just changed directions. She'd see me and start in. What was I doing sitting around reading when there was trash to be taken out and windows to wash? Then she'd start in about how she wasn't our slave. She didn't have to fetch and carry and cook and clean for a bunch of ingrates. God, she didn't cook for David as it was, and we'd been doing our own laundry since we were ten or so."

I put my head in my hands. "I'd try to take David with me sometimes, like out to the park or to the movies, anywhere, just to get him out of her sight, and she'd call my cell. Screaming at me to get David's ass back home. He had to clean his room. I had to mow our lawn. Did I think I could keep everybody else's lawn perfect and our house looking overgrown and abandoned? Did she always have to be the joke of the neighborhood because of her sons?

"I thought I'd get some peace and quiet at school. But if she wasn't calling to bitch about David, David called crying because she wouldn't leave him alone.

And I didn't realize how dark and moody I had gotten. I wouldn't do the frat-boy thing. Wouldn't go hang at the bars because of all the noise. My roommate was a Lit major and nicknamed me Lord Byron, started telling the other guys about my constant phone calls and overhearing someone crying. He asked if I was screwing my sister. I told him I only had a brother and then the gossip went around that I was screwing my brother. Nope, college wasn't the rescue I thought it would be.

"She never let up. It didn't matter that I was out of her sight lines."

I looked back up. "It. Never. Ended."

I pushed my palms against my ears. "I was going out of my mind."

CASS

There's always a deal waiting to be made. That's what Ted always said. It takes the right person to recognize the deal and the time to make it. Could I make a deal with Kyle? Hell yes. I'd done it before. I found the right time and the person to make the deal to become the first junior Homecoming Queen.

"Derek, hey."

"Hey, Cass. Looking great, as always."

Grin/head tilt. "Derek, let's go out and talk a minute." The back-to-school party smelled like beer and sounded like a thunderstorm.

The music followed us out to the pool but I led Derek to the far end, turned, and smiled up at him.

"Cass, as much as I'd like it, I know you didn't bring me out here for a make-out session. What's the deal?"

"Derek. Isn't the football team sick of a band nerd getting Homecoming King every year? Don't you think after sweating through two-a-days, taking your hits on the field, that you deserve that picture in the yearbook? Why does somebody that doesn't do more than get a paper cut from his sheet music deserve the recognition?"

Derek's smile straightened and his jawline hardened. I'd hit the hot button.

I pressed. "I'm sick of it. Homecoming is about football. But band is huge and has to vote for their own nominee for Homecoming Queen. And the Queen's escort is the King."

"And I need a history lesson because?" Derek said.

"Because this is the year to change all that."

"Cass, you have my attention," Derek said.

I didn't need the grin or the head tilt now. I had just sold him his shortcoming. I pulled him down and we sat in the grass. I started ticking the selling points off on my fingers.

"You are the best quarterback our school has had in years. You've got a shot at All State. You are the real deal. You have no steady girlfriend. I'm the girl people vote for. I've spent two years getting my name on ballots. People see it enough, they see my face out there enough, I smile enough, and they learn to vote for me. Together, we'll pull in more than double our votes."

"But . . ."

I put a hand on his knee. "Let me finish. Every member of the team votes for me. Not just varsity — JV, sophomore, freshman, all those teams. And, the word goes out that any team member with a girlfriend has that girlfriend vote for me. It's his duty to do that for his varsity quarterback. Now think about that a minute, Derek."

Derek's brow furrowed, then he looked at me like he saw the sun rise. "A lot of those girlfriends are in band."

"Yes, they are. We not only consolidate votes among the football teams, which you guys haven't been doing, we steal votes from the band. And you, Derek, will be the Homecoming King. The varsity quarterback. The way it should be." I had just wrapped it up in a bow.

"But what about us? The you-and-me kind of us?"

"We have a good time. We date, go to the things where we'll be seen. If you want to see someone else on your private time, that's cool. After Homecoming, you don't have to be stuck with me. This is all for what should be, and yes, so I have something nice for my résumé. But, personally, I'm tired of the band thinking Homecoming is their private territory."

Derek stood and helped me up. He hugged me then put out his right hand to shake on it.

"We've got a deal, Cass McBride."

If I could sell Derek, I could sell Kyle. Where was Kyle? It had to be Saturday and it had to be late. Kyle must have gone home for the night. It was night and I was alone in this box and no one knew where I was.

So I lost it. This time not to panic, but to sorrow. I didn't think I had any tears left but they came. And grief lives right in the middle of your chest. Your heart doesn't break; it dissolves, leaks away, and it hurts. It hurts.

I wanted my mom. I wanted her to hold me and stroke my hair off my forehead and sing that Cajun nursery song that she sang when I had a bad dream. I wanted to hug her and smell her shampoo, not dirt and urine.

A hot wad of pain in my left calf interrupted my self-pity. The muscle was knotted hard. Charley horse? Think. Pull your toes back, not forward.

Hard. Pull hard. I anchored my heel on the coarse surface. God, that hurt. I couldn't reach my toes with my fingers so I had to force my muscles to pull my toes back.

I would win against this pain.

Cass McBride gets what she wants.

I forced my heel down harder and my toes back more.

My back muscles were rigid. From forcing my toes? Because I'd been in one position so long? My throat was tight.

Panic now. Like a big black vulture spreading his wings over me, hovering. Always there, waiting for me.

I screamed. Shredding my throat yet again. I scrabbled and clawed at the top of the coffin and thrashed back and forth, banging my shoulders against the sides of the box. The crate, Kyle called it.

God, I had to calm down. Stop. Please, please stop, Cass.

I had to live through this night.

Could I sleep? Would I wake up again? How do you sleep when you keep panic away with pain?

No, I couldn't sleep.

But, I would calm down.

What was that song my mother sang?

Front, petit front

Yeux, petits yeux

Nez de croquant

. . .

Quiriquiqui

I would sing that song. I would breathe in and out.

I would live through this night.

BEN

"Tell me you guys have something," Ben said.

The four uniforms assigned to the case sprawled in aluminum chairs around a battered table.

The first officer up glanced at his notes. "School counselors all came and started calling kids that knew the girl. The counselors told the kids they phoned to put out the word to anyone they knew that might have information or just wanted to tell us something about Cass to come by the school. Saturday makes it hard, but we got a whole boatload of kids. Some just wanted attention; a few wanted to be someplace besides home; some get off on being part of the action, right? But ya never know. Summarizing seven hours of listening to all her 'really good friends,' Cass McBride was: stuck-up, the friendliest girl in school, a bitch, an angel, too rich for her own good, generous to a fault, a slut, an ice princess, outgoing, shy, totally unstable, knew what she wanted and how to get it, smart, dumb as patio furniture; and whatever happened, she deserved because she treated people like crap, or else she didn't deserve anything like this because she gets along with everyone." He flipped his notebook closed. "Same old, same old. If she gave the talker the time of day, they loved her; if not, Cass was bad news on a biscuit."

The officer frowned and flipped his notes open again. "Oh, Susan Allison, wants to be called Firefly, weird haircut, earrings as big as golfballs, all that black-and-white makeup stuff, says she's pretty sure Cass was pregnant."

"Pregnant?" Ben asked.

"Pregnant. *Firefly* reports catching Cass in an early-morning hurl a couple of days ago."

Ben was marking a dry-erase board. "Guessing Cass and Firefly weren't friends?" He wrote *pregnant* on the board. "We won't spend time on this now. We can ask the best friend. But my gut tells me no."

He pointed to the board. "Leatha. She makes sense. I think Cass is how she describes her to be. But that leaves us with a big nothing."

Ben looked at the clock. At the crime board. Back at the clock.

"We're past the first twenty-four and we've got nothing?"

KYLE

"I don't know why I didn't figure out that David would pick Cass when we made the plan. I mean, you've seen her. Doesn't she look sort of like an old, hard version of Cass? And she knew who Cass was. She was always asking for our school newspaper and checking out the local rags and Cass was always there. She'd either tell us over and over again about how she used to be just like that, only she was a cheerleader to boot. She was popular in high school, she was always in the paper, she was Miss Wonderful. Or she'd rant that Cass had a father who made a decent living. Cass had a father that people respected. Cass's family belonged to the country club. Cass was a child to be proud of. Cass didn't lurk around in shadows. Cass wasn't an embarrassment.

"Why didn't I see it coming? But I didn't. I never thought David would aim that high."

I could almost hear her in my head asking the question I didn't want to hear. *Who told David to aim high? And who taught him to climb that tree?*

CASS

"Still there?"

Fear had worn me down, and this raging thirst had tired me, but his taunt lit my fuse. This was a game of wits now.

"I'm here."

"I'm disappointed. I thought you'd be screaming or at least crying. Afraid I wouldn't come back?"

I fisted my left hand, but kept myself together. Was it still Saturday? Was it Sunday? How was I supposed to figure out time? "You stayed away a little too long and missed all that." I sighed loud enough for the radio. "I'm screamed out. Cried dry. I figure I can't do shit but wait. For you to show up or me to die." I paused for a long beat. "You're holding all the cards, right?"

He paced across me. Static came from the radio and he didn't say anything. He hadn't expected that. Good.

"Burying somebody alive pretty much guarantees you the edge," Kyle said.

My heart squeezed again. Never underestimate your opponent. I tried to convince myself that I wasn't in a box, in a grave. I was lying on the ground under the night sky, eyes closed.

When I felt the blood finally begin to pump again, I thought, *Don't beg; don't demand. Make your voice say "I respect you."* "Are you going to do all the talking or can I ask you anything?"

"That depends on the questions," he said. Those were the words. His tone said — *Don't push me.*

"First, can I say his name?" Good girl, Cass — get permission, make him think he's in charge. I licked my lips. So dry.

"Bitch, I *want* you to say his name. *David.* He's not a nobody you scrape off the bottom of your shoe. That's why you're here. He's a person and you treated him like dirt and now he's dead."

The sudden flash of his hatred startled me. I knew

he was crazy, but his brand of crazy had seemed — cold and calculating. This was instability and that was a lot more dangerous. I gulped in the air again. Slow.

Slow.

Slow.

"I hear you . . . and there's no reason to mess around with anything but the truth. And I know that I must be responsible for David." Kyle was quiet. I seized the moment and went on. "And I'm as self-centered as you say I am, but I didn't know David."

"You didn't *want* to know him."

I waited a few seconds and mellowed my voice to smooth and conciliatory. "He asked me out, I told him that I was busy. I wrote a crappy note. He found it and I'm sorry that happened. But I didn't know I was anything but a blip on his radar. I didn't know I could be that important to anyone."

"Don't feed me this Miss Innocent shit."

I gave Kyle another cooldown moment.

"I want you to tell me about David."

I waited. He wasn't talking. I breathed a little deeper. Calmed down. "I don't believe you would do something like . . . *this*. You've got to think I deserve it. If I did that kind of . . . damage, then I . . . well, I don't know what to think. I need to know something about David before I can understand how I did this to him. Can you explain it for me?"

He punched on the radio but didn't talk. Static. The white noise told me a lot.

Finally. "I won't tell you to help you feel better. I'll do it to make you suffer."

I didn't care why the bastard talked. As long as he kept it up.

And I'll keep agreeing with you, Kyle, as long as you give me something to use. I know what my fear is. I need to know yours.

He didn't speak for a long time. Too long. He needed a nudge.

"I don't want to pry into anything that's just between you and David, okay?"

Nothing.

"But I heard he left a note."

"David left a note all right. And the note is all about why you're in that box."

The anger had flashed and was cold now.

"The cops took it, but left us a copy. To see if we could make sense of it.

"They didn't need to leave a copy. I'll never forget a word. See what *you* think David meant."

The radio clicked off. Was he crying now?

Or struggling not to?

The walkie came back on.

"It wasn't addressed to anyone. He wrote it on copy paper with a marker. Black. Medium tip. Neat block letters. Easy to read. Nothing all drama queen—like, scrawled in messy letters in his own blood. He even used a safety pin — a *safety* pin — to attach it to a hunk of his chest. Went right through the skin and some fatty tissue with the prong and back out and clipped the point into the capped end. That's David, orderly and precise. Didn't want to let that note flap away in the wind."

The radio clicked off again.

Why? Kyle *was* struggling. His emotions were frayed and close to the surface. He didn't want me to know.

Weakness.

My enemy's weakness is my advantage.

But, I had underestimated him before. If I pushed too hard or too fast, he might just walk away.

The walkie popped to life:

WORDS ARE TEETH.
AND THEY EAT ME ALIVE.
FEED ON MY CORPSE INSTEAD.

BEN

"Tyrell, you get anything . . . ?" Ben wiggled his fingers in the air like spider feet.

Tyrell shook his head. "Nah, no weird vibes. Talk to Roger about insects."

"Arachnids," Roger said.

"Gesundheit. Anyway, all I got are guys that got shot down. Girls who were jealous. Girls who wished they could be her. That's it. That whole school's a mess. Remember the suicide Tuesday? Then a kidnapping on Friday."

"Right, I got that too," Roger said. "The whole heebie-jeebies thing. Nobody sees a connection, though."

"We'll come back to that." Ben jabbed a finger at Roger. "Go."

"I talked to the teachers. I've got a good tape from an English teacher I want you to hear. For the rest of Cass's teachers, they all see her the same. Driven. Say she smiles and compliments and says the right things. But the smart ones say they feel manipulated, hmmm, 'worked,' one of them put it. But she's a good student, organized, assignments prepared and on time. No discipline problems. Well dressed and turned out. Pleasant. Yada yada. The kind you recommend to universities, but never feel close to. But the history teacher . . ." He trailed off.

"What?"

"History teacher was a mess. Said this was the second time in a week the cops had been to see him. The kid that killed himself had been in one of his classes too."

Ben sat forward. "Did she —"

"Know him?" Roger finished. "In class with him, but the teacher, a coach, said they didn't travel in the same circles. Said the boy flew too low for her radar. For anybody's radar, really. He didn't think Cass would know his name except for when they had a moment of silence in class for him the day his death was announced."

"We need to —"

"I already checked into the kid. David Kirby. Death officially suicide. No hint of foul play. Note pinned to the kid's body. Talked to the investigating officer. Said the mother was the one that needed hanging. A piece of work. I called McBride and asked if Cass knew the Kirby kid. He said no. He didn't even know about the kid's death. Said Cass didn't go to a funeral. Doesn't look like we've got any connection."

Ben and Roger eyed one another. "But," Ben said.

"But, it feels wrong somehow," Roger answered. "Or maybe right."

Ben looked at the clock. "It's two in the morning. Let's get some sleep and be back here at seven and listen to the teacher's tape."

KYLE

"She didn't want much to do with him. Except when she was ranting at him. He was like a little puppy. Sweet, but I had to watch him all the time. He couldn't take care of himself. Anybody could have killed him with a good kick. I liked taking care of him when we were little.

"But when he got in school he got picked on. He didn't know how to make his way. There's something about a kid who wants too much. Wants people to like him, I mean. School kids whiff that stink of desperation on you and they turn into sharks in a feeding frenzy.

"I wanted to be a cool guy. Stay low, deep, background kind of guy, but I constantly had to rescue David. I was used to it at home, but now he couldn't handle frickin' first graders. I got tired. Always the noise and the crying and talking, and the bitching. I loved David. I loved him. And he needed me. But god help me, he was the cause of all my problems. Well, that's how I saw it then.

"I thought it would get better when I went away to college. But, it didn't. It got so much worse."

CASS

Those words took me right down the rabbit hole.

"Words are teeth . . . eat me alive . . . feed on my corpse"

Tears stung my eyes. How far past bottom does a person have to be to write that? To feel it? David Kirby felt like he was eaten alive? He'd rather be dead than feasted on by people — like me?

For the first time I could remember, I felt sorry for someone other than myself.

"Nothing to say?"

I didn't want to respond but I thought about dirt coming down the air hose. "No," I whispered.

"No?" He whispered too. He seemed next to me in the dark. "No smart remarks? Nothing about the food chain? Don't want to call anyone gay?"

How do you work your way out of something that might actually be your fault?

I felt cold again. From the inside this time. That fleeting feeling that I couldn't handle this, that I wouldn't be able to achieve my goal, was getting less fleeting.

But I wanted to survive.

I still had to try.

It was who I was.

Dad always says that people expect an argument. Anything else catches them unprepared.

"So this is all about two notes. I wrote one that made David write his."

Silence.

"I never thought David would see that note. It wasn't meant to hurt him," I said.

"Don't even start that shit with me."

"I'm not. I know it hurt David and it *is* my fault. I'm not trying to get off the hook. I'm looking back at that day, and you know, with all the stuff that's happened, it changes things."

"Yeah, a few *little* things." It was sarcasm, but it was sadness too. Kyle was doing a piss-poor job of hiding pain. "I have some questions," he said.

"Okay."

"Don't try to mess with me." He sounded like a dog snarling.

"Like you said, you have the edge."

"When did he ask you out?"

"Tuesday. No, Monday. I heard about . . . him on Tuesday."

"How'd he do it?"

I didn't know what he meant. God, Kyle knew what David had done. He'd just told me in horrifying detail.

"I don't understand . . ."

"Ask you out, bitch. How did he do it? Where? What did he say?"

"Oh." I closed my eyes and got a visual of David. "It was in the hall, next to a class we have . . . had together." I told him what I could remember of the conversation. I left out the part about the big ears and the lobe pulling.

"What did you say to him?"

"I was nice. Because I wanted him to vote for me for Prom Queen mostly. I told him I was super busy and I'd get back to him. I smiled at him like it was a real possibility."

"So then what?"

The dark and the cold closed around me. Once I told Kyle, was he going to rip the air tube out and leave?

"Class started."

"Is that when you wrote the note?"

"Yes," I said. "That's when I did it."

I felt and heard something pound above me then. On me. *Slam! Slam! Slam!* I jumped and scrabbled at the top of my coffin with my shredded fingertips. The pounding continued. Faster. Harder.

"What is that? What are you doing?"

One more hard slam.

Kyle's voice was tense and hard. "Why? You told him no. You left him standing there. Why did you write that note? Why did you have to cut him up in pieces like that?"

"I don't know! I don't!" I was screaming. "Stop doing that. What are you doing?" The vibration and the noise, I couldn't . . .

"I'm hitting your grave with the shovel. I wish it was your skull. Tell me. You tell me why you wrote that note."

"I . . ."

I started sobbing. Not fake. Gut-deep kind. Because I had to think about Kyle's question. I saw Dad's face across his desk from me, knocking over my king with his own. And how I'd felt betrayed and . . . insignificant.

"It's twisted, but it's like I can't feel good about me until I put somebody else down. I don't know why I do it. I never thought David would read the note. So, I could feel bigger and it would never touch him."

"You're a piece of shit."

I sighed as more realization swam over me. "Why else would I have to chop everyone else up to feel whole?" Saying it calmed me down. The truth will set you free? Was this as free as I was going to get? Fuck that.

"How did David get the note?" Kyle asked.

I told him.

I expected a stream of cursing. Something, anything but what I got.

A sigh. Of disgust?

"Well, isn't that classic David? As if there's not enough hurt out there with his name on it? No, he's got to go digging to see if he can't find a little more." He sounded sad and tired, but there were feathers of frustration around the edges.

Could I work that?

I wiped my nose and tried to clear my throat with the walkie off, then pressed the button.

"But there's something I don't get . . . ," I said.

Nothing.

"I expected David to show the note to someone. Show people what a shit I was. It's what I would do. If somebody hurts me, I take it back to them, you know?"

"Not everybody is like you."

"But you are," I said, keeping the words as soft and easy as I could. "I hurt your brother and you came after me. You took me down. I get that. I do."

113

Footsteps. He paced across my body.

"But, David, he didn't hurt me. He hurt himself. That's what I can't understand. How does anyone do that? And why over a note I wrote? That alone proved I'm a snobby bitch. David had to be smart enough to know that."

He kept pacing.

I kept talking.

"I didn't know David. For you to do — this — then he had to be special. He can't have been a loser. You said he wasn't a nobody. So he had to see me for what I am. You do."

"Shut up!"

There.

There it was.

Kyle lost control.

This time it wasn't *at* me. It was *to* me. All the difference in the world.

I knew it was momentary. He was still up there and I was down here, but it was the first skirmish where I had taken the edge. Now I had to hold it.

"Sure," I said. "Shutting up."

"Give it a rest. You're just like her, you know.

You never shut up. Yammering in our heads and there's no . . ." He trailed off.

What the hell was he talking about? Her who?

"You want to know about David? Let me tell you about my little brother."

BEN

Ben scrawled David Kirby's name on the board. Scowled. "Roger?"

Roger set up a tape recorder. "This is the best of the interviews I taped. English teacher. Because of scheduling changes this woman taught Cass freshman and sophomore years."

"Let's have a listen," Ben said.

"For the record, this is Cynthia Forman. She teaches at Sterling Valley High School and is speaking for the record with me, Officer Roger Oakley."

"Cass McBride. Yes. You wanted to know about her. Was she popular? That's a word that's not used like we used it when I was in school. Cass

and her friends are what are referred to now as
'résumé packers.' She's wealthy and attractive and,
thankfully, quite intelligent. These RP kids run for
Student Council offices so it looks good for their
extracurriculars. They can't get into a top univer-
sity with just good grades anymore. A girl like Cass
wants to be Prom Queen and Homecoming Queen
and Student Council President to pad out that high
school file and show herself in every possible good
light.

"The kids that aren't competing for the big col-
leges let the RP's take all the prizes. Don't need
it. Don't want it. Don't care. You end up with a
yearbook that shows the same cadre of kids in all
the pictures. Well, they are on the yearbook staff
too. And the real go-getters, like Cass, go beyond
school; they sign up to work for the ASPCA dog
wash and make sure they're there for the photo
shoot. Clean Up the Highway Day – she'll be
there and she'll be in that picture when the paper
comes out.

"Cass isn't as cold as all that sounds. She puts

117

up a good front, but she's just a little girl with her britches hanging out. Oh, I see your face, Officer. Not like that. That's an old Southern expression, meaning she's showing things she doesn't know she shows.

"In our poetry unit Cass turned in interesting work. Here, let me read one for you:

I climb the sheer wall of my father's
    expectation
While his determination of the greatness
    that I'll achieve
Tells of the nothing he knows me now to be
The steepness attracts
Draws me
Though there is no soft place to fall,
Not to climb
Will leave me in the cold.

"I was never much good with poetry, but all that stuff about her father's 'expectation,' does that sound any alarms for you?"

"Officer, your mind went to the gutter again. No,

I don't think there is sexual abuse in that house. But Ted's love for Cass is conditional. Somewhere deep down, she knows that. It makes me sad for her. I know, sad for the poor little rich girl. How trite.

"*Who do I think took her? That's unfathomable. Her father is wealthy, but not that wealthy. Let's hope the kidnappers think he is and she's alive.*"

"Good work, Roger. All that kind of knits together with the poetry book we found in the girl's nightstand." He stared at the board. "The kid has issues with her father but I don't see it leading anywhere in this kidnap, do you?"

He surveyed the officers and then struck a line through Ted McBride's name.

"I saved you for the good stuff," Ben said to the female officer.

"The friends," she said. "All but the boyfriend and the best friend. Those two are waiting for you in the interview rooms."

Her notebook was open but she didn't glance

at it. "There's a crowd of girls that hang with her on a regular basis. All affluent parents. High-end homes and cars. Great clothes, uptown haircuts, rich-kid lifestyle. A couple have been busted for small-time possession. No bigs, and Daddy's lawyers smoothed it over. Not bad kids, really. No huge trust funds to keep them rich forever so they'll have to go to school to maintain their privileged lifestyle. Keeps 'em honest.

"Guys are the same way. Pretty decent. When you get past the posturing, I got the same story. Cass doesn't see high school boys as anything but a staging area. Practice. If I'm reading her right, she dates the football captain during football season, the basketball star during that season."

Tyrell whistled. "An athletic supporter."

She sighed. "I have a gun and I *will* use it."

He put up his hands in surrender.

"You know what I think it means?" the officer said.

Ben nodded. "She's a teenager."

"That's how I see it."

"Tyrell, go see the teachers and the principal about the Kirby kid. I don't like coincidence. And that's a big one. Then put the squeeze on forensics about the drug tests," Ben said. He stared at the board. "We're running out of time."

KYLE

I pressed my palms against my ears. Trying to keep the sound out. But the sounds were *in* my head. I squeezed my eyes shut and tried not to think but the voice wouldn't go away. The voice over the phone. The voice in my ear the night I made the plan.

"She's tearing me apart, Kyle. Come home; it's not so bad when you're here."

"Just keep out of her way, David, you can . . ."

"I can't. You know how she is."

"I know. I hear you and I know." I paced the room, listening to David's ragged breathing in my ear. Pulled the cell phone away so I could think. It was barely October and this year was already worse than last. Mom was

worse to David when I was away at school than when I was home.

What could David do that . . .

I put the phone back to my ear. David was crying again. "David, stop crying and listen. I've got an idea. Maybe we can shut her up for good."

CASS

"It starts with her."

"Her? What starts with her?" I asked.

"Pay fucking attention! You want to know about David? It starts with her. My mother. I guess a shrink would say it starts with her mother and then her mother and back until a woman in a cave clonked her daughter on the head with a club. Like I give a shit. That's ancient history."

He stopped talking, but the static hissed and crackled. Kyle was in a rage.

"My mother was the blond cheerleader, Homecoming Queen, parasitic *bitch* that didn't intend to work for a living."

Even knowing Kyle was a nutcase, that sudden

lash of spite startled me. How could I outmaneuver a full-fledged, mother-hating psychopath?

"She was determined to nab the football star that was headed to medical school. He was scholarship material all the way, so there would be no putting a husband through med school. Not for her. Nope — spend a few years living the young college life and then coast in the rich lane with DR. WIFE vanity plates on a Jag."

His radio popped off. I couldn't feel him walking. I guess he was standing still. Thinking? Deciding what to say next?

He needed a prompt.

"I'm guessing the football player/med student was your dad?"

"No shit, Sherlock."

"You're telling me that your mom married your dad just so she could be a doctor's wife? Not because she loved him?"

"That's what I'm telling you."

I stayed quiet. I tried to move my legs. My knees were stiff and aching and I groaned as I eased them out a bit. "When I read about David in the news-paper, it didn't say your dad was a doctor."

Kyle made a sound I think was supposed to pass for a laugh. It didn't come close. "He's not.

"I was Mom's snare to get Dad," Kyle said. "She wasn't worried when he didn't want to get married right out of high school, but when he finished undergrad work and got into medical school, she saw the writing on the wall. She didn't like the story."

Static. Something. Maybe a sigh.

"Mom took action. The wedding was rushed, but Mom was happy. She was happy with me. I was the key to the lock that kept Dad as her treasure chest."

Kyle seemed to be waiting for a reaction.

"That sucks," I said.

Slam! Slam! Slam!

The shovel again.

"Shut up!" Kyle shouted.

BEN

"You don't seem worried," Ben said.

"Nothing to hide. Why would I worry?"

A young man lounged in the chair, seemingly unconcerned about being interviewed by the police. Arrogant and handsome, he bored Ben and crawled right up Scott's neck.

"You're dating a girl that's missing. You're not worried about her safety?" Ben said.

The kid sighed. "Nobody really dates Cass. She sort of allows you to take her places."

Ben sat back, a signal for Scott to take over.

"I gotta tell you, that would spin me up a little. What do you mean, 'allows you to take her places'?"

Derek Richards smiled. "It's not like that. She's pretty and she never dates anybody for a long time, so you know not to get, like, invested. But, she's fun and can be funny and it feels good to be seen with her. It's a win-win deal."

Scott walked behind Derek. "We heard she can be kind of a backbiter."

"Maybe. She might make fun of the nobodies and the dorks. But I've never heard her say anything mean about, you know, *us*."

Scott made a gun out of his finger and thumb and mimed shooting Derek in the back of the head. "Never talked shit about the people that count, right?" He circled around to face the young man.

Derek smiled. "Right."

Ben and Scott exchanged glances. The kid was a bonehead.

"So, you're telling me, you, nor anybody else that dated Cass, would want to put the grab on her?"

Derek smirked. "Put the grab? You're trying too hard. Give it up and just talk like an old guy. I can translate. No, I have no reason to kidnap Cass and I don't think anybody else that went out with her would either. It's not Cass's way to make enemies with boyfriends. She doesn't let you get that close, you know what I mean? She keeps it loose."

Ben interrupted. "I think we get the picture. Did you know David Kirby?"

Derek put his palms up and out. "Whoa, the train jumped the tracks there. David Kirby? The kid that offed himself?"

Ben stared the kid down, long enough to send a message.

"Don't get all righteous on me. I didn't know him. I know his brother. By rep anyway. He's a year older and we didn't hang together. Until what's-his-name died, I didn't know Kyle Kirby *had* a brother."

"So David Kirby was one of those people that didn't count," Scott said.

"Hey, I'm, like, volunteering to talk to you, and you're going for attitude. I didn't know David Kirby. Kyle Kirby, I knew a little. He played baseball. He dated hot girls. But, you know, he was kind of like Cass. He was 'seen' with them. I don't remember him having a girlfriend. And he was weird about something else."

"What was that?" Ben asked.

"Summers. The dude worked. Landscaping. Yard work. I mean, it kept him ripped, but . . . well, that meant he couldn't hang with all the guys. Kirby was a loner."

"What do the 'other' guys do in the summer?" Scott asked.

"Sports camp. Work out at the gym. Hang. You know."

Ben stood. "You can go." He walked Derek past Scott, who glared the kid out the door.

"I'm trying too hard?" Scott said when Ben returned. "Talk like an old guy?"

Ben rubbed his chin, trying to hide his grin. "It happens to all of us."

"What? What happens?" Scott demanded.

"We find out we're not cool."

"I *am* cool. That kid was the product of poor toilet training. I am cool."

"I stand corrected. Let's talk to the best friend."

KYLE

"I didn't come home much the first year I was in college. I managed to avoid Thanksgiving by going camping with an Eco Friends group, so it was Christmas before I saw David. Since that September he must have lost fifteen pounds, and he didn't have it to lose. He looked tired and listless and kept his head down and answered in monotones around Mom."

I got him alone in our room. "What the hell is going on?"

He started crying. "It's worse than ever. I could take it when you were here. Dad stays gone all the time and now she doesn't stop. She just keeps going off on me. For anything. For nothing. I can't think. I can't study. My grades are shit and that makes her mad. I have to come straight home from school and go to my room. No TV. She moved the computer downstairs and I can't use it unless she sits right behind me to make sure I'm doing school stuff. She comes in and out of my room to 'check' on me, but she stays there and tells me that I'm lazy, that I'm just like Dad, that I give up rather than stick with something, that I'm stupid. You've heard it all, just multiply by about a hundred."

David curled into fetal position.

"I'll do something," I said. "I don't know what. But I'll take care of this."

"You can't," he said. "Nobody can."

But I tried. Dad took off the day after Christmas; we didn't even ask what trip or where and even why he needed to sell drugs during the holidays. I cornered Mom with her morning coffee.

"Mom, you need to let up on David."

"David isn't your concern."

"He's my brother."

She raked her fingers through her hair, massaging her temples. "If I hadn't birthed him myself, I'd find it impossible to believe."

"That's the kind of stuff I'm talking about, Mom. You have to stop saying shit like that."

She glared at me, but I locked on to the glare with my own. Something flickered and her bottom lip softened slightly and she looked away, like she was bored.

"A semester of college and you think you know it all. You don't know crap."

"Then tell me. Tell me why you do this to him. And don't give me that BS about David ruining your life. He didn't do anything to you. The kid got born. That wasn't his fault. That was your fault. Yours and Dad's."

Mom pulled back as if I'd slapped her.

"You don't understand. You're still young and have it all in front of you. You read, you think, you make good grades, and you know what you want. David could do that too. But he's wasting it. He's just throwing it away. Like his father did. Just like I did. I can't stand seeing it."

"Mom —"

"What happened to this family when life got tough? Your father caved. He just quit. And he's been quitting ever since. He's a loser and I can't leave him because I don't know how to make it on my own. I got to graduation with

133

*the best boyfriend but with C's and D's and no skills at all.
It was more important to condition my hair and do my nails
than homework. I worried more about how to cross my legs so
my butt looked good than about what the teacher might be
saying. My mother married well and all she taught me was
how to do the same thing. Well, it turns out I didn't even
marry well!*

*"David's just like your father. He won't stand up and
fight. He has to toughen up. This world is going to walk all
over him if he doesn't learn to get tough. He's a crybaby
and he has to get over it. You're not helping him, Kyle. You
think you're protecting him from me, and from the bullies
at school, but you're just making him weak."*

*"Do you love David? Tell me the truth, Mom. Do you
love David at all?"*

"I do what I have to do," she said.

"I wondered if she might be right. Was I making
David weaker?

"And Mom thought it was her job to make him
tough.

"One thought nagged me. While Mom didn't love
David, did she love her 'job' a little too much?"

CASS

Kyle pounded the shovel again.

If I could get out of this crate, I would send every one of Kyle's teeth flying with one good whack of that shovel and then cram it down his newly excavated mouth.

My head hurt and I felt like shit. And it was hard to think about anything but how thirsty I was. I couldn't get it right all the time. It was so hard to concentrate.

"Mom was getting what she wanted, but Dad was having a hard time. And then a mistake happened. David. Two kids were more than Dad could handle with med school. He quit."

I learned my lesson and stayed quiet. I think the pauses were Kyle deciding what to tell me, how much of my talking he could tolerate. That was important to know.

"And Mom didn't get to be a doctor's wife. Dad's a pharmaceutical rep. Yup, he peddles drugs. Legal ones, of course. Not quite what Mom had planned. And in her mind, it was all David's fault. He crashed her party. The way I see it, Dad never had what it takes to be a doctor, but Mom refuses to believe she misjudged him so far back. And Dad is still her paycheck. She can't be mad at him, so she gets twice as mad at David. And here's the deal. I look like Mom. David looks like Dad.

"Life handed David a heaping pile of shit, and no matter how deep he dug, he was never going to find a pony."

Kyle went quiet for a bit. Wandering down memory lane, I guess. I wiggled around a little. I didn't think I could say anything right now. I'd wait him out. I arched my back, but it seized up and cramped. I was getting colder and stiff. Kyle still wasn't talking. I had to take a chance.

"How do you know all this stuff? That she got

136

pregnant with you to trap your dad? That she blamed David for your dad not being a doctor?"

That sound that was supposed to be a laugh. "I think my mother was always mean, but she covered it up with cute when she was young. So she could get what she wanted. But when cute faded away, mean was all she had left. You understand?"

I thought about my head tilt/grin. What would I have when I wasn't young enough to carry that off? The idea of Dad needing me to be a McBride to marry well . . .

"I don't have a dress," Mom said.

Dad had just shown us an invitation. He was Businessman of the Year. Small pond, big fish, but he was strutting anyway.

"Leatha, I know you hate these things. Don't bother. Cass will go with me," he said.

I watched, knew a moment was here. Mom locked eyes with Dad. She broke first and turned away. It was done. Dad had chosen sides. Picked the team, but I could change it. I could . . .

Dad handed me his Visa. "Sky's the limit," he said. "Make your old dad look good."

I kept losing focus. I was too slow processing information.

Then it hit me.

"She *told* you?"

"Oh, she told me. Over and over and over. I think she was drunk the first time, but usually she wasn't. She told me when she was pissed, and when she was feeling sorry for herself. And she told David. Told him that he was the reason Dad wasn't a doctor, but practically a traveling salesman, and that was why she wasn't invited to join the country club, and David was the reason we don't live in the 'best' neighborhood, and David was the reason her life was a social and financial disaster."

"Oh." I whispered it. What did I write in the note? *How low on the food chain . . .*

"Yeah, oh."

"Was she mean to you? Or just to David?"

The question stopped him again. I waited him out.

"She was screwy about it. Sometimes she would . . . play us off each other, or . . ." Silence again.

"There's so much stuff, it gets hard to remember — but one that stands out was prom my senior year. I came down the stairs in my tux. Mom was on the sofa with David. She was reading comics with him. She usually called him a geek about his comics. Threw them away just to screw him over. But she had bought him, like, five comics and they were reading them together. David was smiling so hard he was glowing.

"Mom looked at me. 'Well, don't you clean up nice.' But I heard something dark in her voice, knew there was something coming that I didn't want to hear.

"'All dressed up so you can get in some slut's pants? Isn't that what happens at the prom? Don't think I don't know what goes on.'

"She had to make sure she ruined it. Nobody was going to be happy around her. But she wanted to make sure she had David on her side when she broadsided me.

"I wondered if she was smart enough to know that she had to give David a little bit of affection here and there — the carrot on the string — to keep him coming back. It had to hurt him more when she tore into him right after she'd been kind. So once in a while she'd say 'Hi, David, how was your day? Come tell me about it.' Or give him a hug. That way he'd keep coming back, thinking *this* time, maybe this time she would love him just a little."

He lowered his voice. Almost confessional. "I knew better. She couldn't love him. It would never happen.

"And most of the time just seeing him set her off. She'd go off and it would move over onto me. 'Why can't you keep him out of my sight?' That was what she'd scream at me the most. 'How useless are you that you can't keep a worm like this underground?' And sometimes . . . shit, sometimes I'd wish he hadn't been born. What's that make me?"

There! I had it. Kyle had given me his self-doubt and I could sell it back to him. He believed he hadn't loved his brother enough, that he hadn't protected him enough, and that's what really killed David.

Not *me.*

My mouth was so dry that talking was getting hard, but I had what I needed. I had to use it.

"It makes you a human being. One that was

manipulated since you were a little kid. I mean, I think so."

Nothing.

"Kyle, let's look at just the facts here. You buried me alive. That makes me think you're not a good person. Then you tell me that your mother is horrible, made David feel like shit all his life. And you get mad at him because you got the fallout. Sure, that makes you a shit-head.

"But, and here's the biggie, the little bit you have said sounds like your mother is a person that's all about herself. So, I can't see her being Cuddle Mom to you. She had to be doing a number on your head. When did you first catch on?"

Ted's Rule Two: Ask the leading question. If Kyle answered, I had a chance to keep the game in play.

BEN

"Erica Lambert?"

The girl was pretty and poised. Dark hair and eyes, but no hard edges, no false bravado like the moron that had preceded her.

"One of our medical examiners —"

"Is my mother," Erica said.

Ben arched the eyebrow. "I know her. She's good at what she does."

"She's good at lots more," Erica said.

"Cass McBride."

Erica's eyes filled but didn't overflow. She straightened her spine, folded her hands, and composed herself. "What do you need to know?"

"Who would take her?"

"If I had any idea, you would know by now."

Ben tapped a pencil against the desk.

"Tell me about her. What's she like? Anything."

"She's my best friend."

"Tell me something about her that would piss her off if she knew you said it," Ben said.

Erica's face registered the shock. "Why would you want me to do that?"

"Singing her praises doesn't tell me who would take her. Unless you know about a stalker, and you'd have already told me that. So give me a not-so-great quality; maybe that will lead me somewhere."

Her voice was low when she began and she didn't make eye contact. "Cass has a wicked sense of humor, but it's usually aimed at someone. But behind their back. She doesn't hurt anyone's feelings — you know, to their face." Erica paused. Looked up. "It sounds bad. I know. But it's high school. It's what people do. And Cass is so good at seeing stuff in people, little things to pull out and exaggerate. She did these dead-on impersonations at parties. We couldn't help laughing. But sometimes it could be mean and I wished then she'd lighten up."

"Did she make enemies that way?" Ben asked.

"Guys, never. Cass was careful; if she did a take on a guy where anyone could see or hear, it was funny, but not so that it would embarrass the guy. It was almost a compliment. She could get a little bitchier with girls. But I don't know anybody that had a real hate going for Cass."

"Were you and Cass close enough for her to give you intimate details of her life?"

Erica blushed. "Are you talking about sex?"

Ben gave her one curt nod.

"I know she's a virgin."

"So if I told you someone told us she might be pregnant, you would say what?"

"I would say you were listening to someone that's stupid or has an agenda."

"Okay, changing subjects. Did you know David Kirby?" Ben asked.

Erica's head had been lowered, studying her hands as if she was embarrassed to criticize her friend. Her eyes seemed to pull her head up, slow, wondering, almost frightened. Ben sensed a secret.

Ben leaned forward.

"David Kirby?" Erica said, "what's he got to do with this? I mean, he's dead. He died before Cass was kidnapped. She was kidnapped, right? You asked who would take her?"

"Erica," Ben said, "what do you know about Cass and David Kirby?"

"Nothing." She looked at Ben then back at Scott. "Honestly, it's nothing. My mom got the call about him. She told me about it, because she thought I might know him. Didn't want me to be surprised if it was announced at school. I told Cass and she . . ." Erica faltered and a crease dug between her eyes as she stared into her lap.

"What, Erica?" Ben gentled his voice, leading the girl.

She put her index finger on the crease between her eyes and rubbed. Easing it, she lifted her eyes.

She doesn't know she does it, Ben thought. It's a decision to tell the truth.

"She surprised me. I thought she'd blow it off or make the proper noises or ask the gruesome questions that people ask me, you know, because of my mom."

Ben nodded.

"But, she went all —" She stopped. The crease. The look down. The rub. Back up. "She looked *scared*. I can't remember ever seeing Cass scared. Then she ran to the bathroom and threw up."

"She barfed?" Scott said.

Ben closed his eyes and gritted his teeth.

But Erica responded to Scott. She turned to face him. "Right in a sink. Didn't make it to the toilet. I couldn't believe it. It was so embarrassing, but more than that, it was so NOT Cass."

"Was there a girl called Firefly in the bathroom when that happened?" Scott had a feeling he'd engaged the girl and ran with it.

Erica nodded. "Oh, that's who you're talking about. About Cass being pregnant." She sighed and rolled her eyes up. "She asked Cass if she was knocked up or hung over."

Ben mentally crossed *pregnant* off the crime board.

"Cass say anything about hurling?" Scott asked.

Erica nodded again. "She said she got a 'visual'

and it made her stomach go wonky. She said she thought she had a class with David."

"Thought?"

"Right. She wasn't sure. David didn't sail in Cass's ocean. She didn't even know he was Kyle Kirby's brother."

Ben interrupted. "Cass knew the brother?"

"Knew of. We both kind of crushed on him when we were freshmen. He didn't know we were on the planet."

"After she threw up, how did she act after that?" Scott asked.

"Just like the old Cass. It was a bump in the road. But it was a weird bump."

"She didn't go to the kid's funeral, right?" Scott said.

"No, I did. My mom and I went. His dad is a pharmaceutical rep. I didn't know it, but he brings new stuff to the office so they have it for testing. Honestly, that's the only reason I knew Kyle and David were brothers. Because Mom knows their dad."

"Okay, what about old boyfriends? Any of those holding a grudge?"

"Not the boyfriends." She rubbed the crease in her forehead again. "Let me give you an example. Right now, Cass will be the Homecoming Queen. She has been dating Derek Richards because he's a senior and the starting quarterback. That helped her get all the football team votes because that will make Derek the Homecoming King." Erica looked at Ben then Scott. "Following?"

"King is the guy who is the Queen's date. He doesn't get elected," Scott said.

"Right. Now, Jen Underwood is, like, crazy in love with Derek, so she's totally jealous of Cass."

"So you think this Underwood kid would take Cass to keep her from getting Homecoming Queen?"

Erica grimaced. "No. You guys watch too much TV. Jen Underwood knows that the minute Homecoming is over, Cass won't be dating Derek anymore. In fact, Cass will probably talk Jen up to Derek during the Homecoming dance. Jen will end up with Derek because of Cass and she might not have had a chance with him before. That's why nothing bad ever sticks to Cass."

Scott rubbed his head. "Then what happens to Cass?"

"She dates here and there. No more than a date or two with any guy. When she gets a handle on who is most likely to be Prom King, she'll date him until prom is over."

"And then Cass will hand him off to someone that's in love with him?"

"Probably. That's why I don't understand this. It has to be someone who doesn't know her. Someone who wants her dad's money. But my dad says her father is in hock up to his ears." Erica stopped. "I shouldn't have said that."

Ben rocked back in his chair. "Oh, yes, you should."

KYLE

"The phone calls never stopped from either of them."

"David, David, calm down. I can't understand you when you're crying. Okay, yeah. What'd she do? Yeah, that's shitty. Dad out of town? Sure, he's always out of town. I get it, David. You can't do your homework if she's in your room screaming and calling you stupid all the time, and if you can't do your homework you make shitty grades. None of that's new. I hear you. Okay. Listen, send me the assignment for your English paper; e-mail it to me and I'll . . . oh, right, she sits right there with you. Do we have time for me to snail mail it to you? Okay, that's no good. Damn, she goes through every piece of your mail?"

"I couldn't stand it. I needed to come up with something to shut them both up."

"Mom? You're yelling and it's hard for me to . . . No, I wasn't planning to come down this weekend. But . . . Mom, if you would leave David alone for a few hours every night so he could get his homework done, he . . . It's not a matter of taking sides . . . Well, it's hard to get any studying done if someone is talking to you . . . I know, Mom. I'm not there and I don't understand what David puts you through, but . . . I know; I've got it good up here. No worries; just me and my books, you and Dad paying all my bills. I know, I'm ungrateful and I should come home and take some of the burden from your shoulders. No, I'm not mocking you. I can't do anything right; I can't say anything right around you, Mom. Neither can David. I wish you would leave him alone a little, just . . . Mom?

I know Mom gave me that whole speech about wasting her time concentrating on the social parts of school, but that was bullshit. She hated David because he was a dweeb. I skated by because I was more socially acceptable. I knew what David had to do to make her happy and grabbing a wad of A's wasn't the answer.

I told David what to do. What to say. I didn't tell him who to pick but I did tell him what type to choose. I told him what shirt to wear, which shoes, what pants, the whole works. I pumped him up, told him how it would work out fine. It would be cruise control the whole ride. I reminded him of how I taught him to climb the tree in front of our house. How he could reach higher than he thought."

I shook my head. "He called me Monday. Late. Ten, maybe a little after."

"Kyle?"

"David, we need to make it quick. I've got a huge test tomorrow." I could hear him breathing over the phone. He wasn't crying. He sounded calm. Thank god.

"Sure, hmmm, I just wanted to thank you, for all your help."

"Oh, did it work out? The date thing?"

"I've got everything set up," David said.

"Good luck, then."

"I couldn't have done it without you. You're a great brother."

"Don't go mushy on me, bro. Just go for it; don't have second thoughts, okay?"

"Sure, go for it."

"Gotta go."

"I love you, Kyle."

"Don't be a dork." I hung up.

"I told him to go for it. Don't have second thoughts."

CASS

Was Kyle really taking this long to answer every question or had I lost all sense of time? Two conflicting things seemed to be happening to me. The air had turned heavier, pushing me down, weighing me down against the bottom of the box. But at the same time, my body seemed to be lighter, like it was drying out into a husk, fragile enough to be blown away, blown apart with a puff of air.

But the husk hurt. My skin felt like it cracked every time I moved, scraping against the linen of my pj's or the rough boards, and my lips bled every time I moved them. And the constant muscle cramps made me move when I didn't want to. I had to work faster. I was losing control of my body. I was losing focus. I was losing track of time. Pretty soon, I'd lose Kyle.

"Catch on?" Kyle said.

What had we been talking about? Think. "Yeah, how old were you when you got the picture that she wasn't Hallmark Mom? That she was the Wicked Witch of the Back Bedroom where David was concerned? That she treated you different?" *Shut up, you're blathering. Let him talk. Don't get amped because you've worked your crowbar into a crack. He'll catch on.*

"Shut up!" he roared into the radio. It filled my black space and shocked me back to exactly where I was. The claustrophobia swamped me and I dragged in breaths rapid and ragged, squeezed my eyes shut, and clenched my muscles to keep from kicking, beating, and screaming. My heart slammed and I wasn't cold now; sweat broke out on my face and neck and warmth flowed along my thighs and —

I had peed myself. An idea. I hit the button and forced a small laugh.

"What the fuck are you laughing at?" He was still pissed.

"At how stupid I am."

Silence. Dad was so right. Agree with someone and they don't know what to say.

"I just peed myself. And you know what was the first thing that went through my head?"

"Oh, I can't live until you tell me." Good, step down from furious to sarcastic.

"I thought, these white pajamas are linen, I'll never get the stain out." I held the button and worked my sob into a laugh. A laugh born of a sob is a dark thing, but it must have fooled Kyle.

"Moron," he said. But the sarcasm wasn't there. He was amused. "First off, you peed yourself before you ever got in the box. The pajamas were already a lost cause."

We both let the irony hang over us. "When you were on the ground, unconscious, I was surprised at something. Your pajamas. Not the all white. But they're man pajamas."

Soft now, almost regretful. Don't alienate him; just plant doubt, but don't push. "You expected . . . what?"

"Are you a lez?"

If nothing else, I wanted to get up out of this box

to kick the shit out of him for being such a dick. I drummed my heels against the bottom of the box so the pain could settle me down.

"That's it, isn't it? That's why you shot David down so bad," he said.

"No. Why do people always go there when . . . forget it. I'm not gay. But I'm not a flash-the-goods-what's-the-highest-offer kind either. I'm not a hottie."

"What are you then?"

This time I was silent. Caught off guard.

"I . . . don't know."

I honestly didn't know. It must be all the dizziness and mind fog that seemed to be setting in.

"I don't want to talk about me. I want to hear about David. You were going to tell me about —"

"When I caught on to Mom. That talking too much, the explaining over and over you did was just like *her*. When she got on something, she wouldn't shut up. On and on, and if David or I left the room, she'd just follow and keep yammering. She did it to Dad too, but he would escape."

"How?"

"Job. Sales reps travel all the time. I'm sure he extended his stays rather than come home."

"He was leaving you two alone with her?"

"Yeah."

"Did he know she was picking on David and screaming at you?"

"He knew."

I waited a minute. Really thinking. Not playing the head game now. Trying to figure out this guy that left his kids alone with a woman so monstrous.

"Um, doesn't that mean he left knowing she was shooting all her bullets into two targets instead of three?"

Nothing.

"And he knew she'd fire most of them into David?"

"You trying to make me hate my father too?"

Soothe. Redirect. "No. You said you were a bad guy because you didn't protect David." *He never said it, but he meant it. If the buyer won't lay his cards face up, the seller has to do it for him.* "But you were a kid. The other adult in your house, your dad, should have been protecting

David. He didn't. He ran away. How were you supposed to protect yourself, much less take care of David?"

Leave him to think a little.

"It must have been hell for you," I said. That shot out of my mouth before I could weigh it for advantages.

"Breakfast."

Breakfast? What brain fart had produced that?

"Not following," I said.

"That's the first time I noticed that she treated us different. Breakfast."

"Oh."

"He had to eat soup," Kyle said.

"I was in third grade and David was in kindergarten. Mom was making pancakes. She put a plate in front of me, poured juice, and ladled scrambled eggs onto my plate and then hers.

"She told David he was on his own.

"He didn't say anything, but he looked from my plate to hers and then at Mom.

"She said she was tired of cooking for him because he complained. She mocked him."

Kyle made his voice high and ugly. A high-pitched whine. 'I don't WHIKE eggs. This pancake isn't a CIRKWUL, it's OOGY.'

Was that supposed to be his imitation of his mother mocking his brother? I was getting mixed up. What would he do if I asked for water? His voice interrupted my thoughts.

"Mom told him that if he didn't like what she cooked, he could fix his own food.

"David had to stand on a chair to look for cereal, but he didn't find any and Mom told him to get tough.

"David pulled out a can of soup with a pop-top. He ate it cold because he didn't know how to use the microwave.

"He ate canned soup for more than a month. Breakfast, lunch, dinner. She tortured him so he'd remember the price of complaining."

"She didn't feed your brother? That's what you're telling me."

"She bought the soup, so it wasn't like she starved him."

I let that dangle a while.

"He dressed really nice," I said.

"Sure, both of us. She liked to shop. And she wanted people to see us wearing good labels. That was about her. Not David."

"He looked, I don't know, uncomfortable in his clothes," I said.

"She'd screech at him, you know?" Kyle's voice rose again. "'I buy you the best and you still look like a loser. Unbutton the top button. Are you too stupid to know how to wear a shirt? Tuck it smooth, don't wad it up, you look like you're carrying a load in those pants. Which you have belted under your armpits for Christ's sake. You could screw up a good dream.' When she caught sight of me, she'd either tell him to catch a clue from me or ask what I was looking at or why wasn't I helping."

His radio clicked off. Then back on. "I can't talk anymore." Off again.

Nothing.

For a long time.

No, no, no. I didn't want to be alone now. I needed him here. I couldn't work him if he wasn't here. Wasn't talking. I had no power over him if he wasn't here. If Kyle was talking, I wasn't thinking about where I was.

I wanted to call out to him but I wasn't sure I wouldn't cry instead. It was almost like I missed him. He was my comfort, the only thing to keep me from being alone, yet he was just out of reach, kind of like my father. God, I was as pathetic as Kyle was.

I got cold. Not chilled cold. Aching cold. Shivers that wouldn't stop. Muscle tremors that turned into full body rattling. Temperature falling? Or was it that I felt it more without words to keep me focused . . . ?

Kyle was gone. I was certain. I didn't think he meant to be gone for good. But could I make it through this cold? How long had I been here?

I pulled my knees in as far as the box allowed, then straightened them. My joints ground against each other. All my joints ached and creaked when I worked them. Is that how dehydration started? My mouth was dry and my tongue felt too big. The headache had to be a bad sign. How do you die of thirst? Would my cells leach the water from my blood?

My chest heaved in a sob, but tears didn't roll. My eyes felt "scritchy." A word my mom always used. She called me "bebe" too, when I was little. Before I decided she was embarrassing.

"What the hell have you done?" Dad was furious.

Mom came in and her eyes registered surprise, but she knelt down to look in my eyes.

"Bebe, you know you're not allowed to use the scissors."

"I don't want bangs anymore. You don't have bangs."

"Look at this mess," Dad shouted. He picked me up and faced me to the hall mirror. A stubble poked from my forehead, the rest of my hair long and flowing. A mess.

"This is your fault, Leatha. Can't you watch a five-year-old, for pity's sake!"

He plunked me down like I was dirty. Wiped his hands against each other. "Forget the company Easter egg hunt. You can't be seen in public like that." He stormed away.

Mom put her arms around me. "Bebe, it's okay, but for some things, like growing out your bangs, you have to wait."

My eyes roamed the nothingness around me. There's no good place to hide in the dark. In the light you can hide from yourself by concentrating on others, deflect attention from your flaws to your strengths or from your flaws to someone else's. I'm a champ there.

The light lets someone see his own airbrushed reflection in you — and that's the best sales pitch ever. Stand in the light and show the audience what they want to be.

But in the dark, it's only you. No shiny reflective surfaces to dazzle, just black holes to stare into and see what you really are.

David Kirby was a suicide waiting to happen. But if my note hadn't pushed him off that limb, hell, who knows? He might have stepped back, talked to a counselor.

But, my words were waiting for David Kirby, left under that desk for anyone to pick up and read.

Sticks and stones may break my bones.

But words will never hurt me.

How much bullshit is that?

And . . . what hurt can an unsaid word do?

Can it be like an antibiotic withheld?

Did Mom leave because of crappy things Dad said or because of things I didn't?

Like, "I understand why you have to go, but please call me." Or, even better, picking up the phone and saying "Hey, Mom, I miss you. I love you. Why don't I come visit?" All that has gone unsaid.

We lie here: me and the box and the dark and the questions.

BEN

A tall man in his early thirties who looked like he'd been assembled of random twigs hunched over a computer monitor.

"You got anything for me?" Ben asked.

The man held up a long finger with knobby knuckles, nosed closer to the screen, then hooked the finger over the bridge of his nose. He slumped against the back of his chair and hit a key. "Printing. Got a ransom call yet?"

"Nope," Ben said.

"Wouldn't do anybody much good. Ted McBride is, indeed, deep in debt. But, it ain't just living above his means. McBride is a savvy businessman. He's got loans against his home and his business, everything but his dog." The knobby-knuckled finger pointed up. "However, and this is a big however, these loans are for his investment in a subdivision for 'adult living.' Like a retirement village. Big business now. You know, for old farts. Well, young farts ought to be investing, but old farts buy the houses." He looked at Ben and shrugged. "He's probably set to make a killing, but right now he's cash poor."

"He got insurance on the kid?" Ben asked.

"Not enough to count. Barely enough for a funeral."

"Any money coming to him through her in case of her death?"

"Nada."

"So . . . ," Ben said.

"It's not about money."

Ben turned to Scott. "We're running out of our first forty-eight and we're going nowhere. Remember Oakley's spider feet about the Kirby kid?"

"Yeah, we talked to everybody and she didn't know the kid."

"But, did he know her?"

Scott scrubbed his spiky hair. "What's to lose?"

KYLE

"So, I thought we had a chance. David would ask some girl out. Someone just like Mom, someone with a bubbly personality. I gave him the lines to make the approach, a few kinda funny things that made him seem a little witty and not so needy, told him exactly what to do.

"And one more time, there wasn't enough hurt sitting on David's shoulder. He goes and finds the biggest hurt he can. Cass McBride."

I dug my nails into my thumbs again. Pain felt so much better than guilt.

"Here's David, thinking it's his last chance, his last chance ever to get Mom to approve of him, and what happens? Cass shoots him down. And she does it by calling him a loser, a bottom-feeder, gay. She rejects him with the same words my mother has."

I wiped the tears from my face. "One thing made me feel a little better. The way David did it. Hanging himself so publicly. In front of our house, with that note on his chest. It told me something.

"David finally worked up the nerve to . . ." I looked at the cops. "The kid just royally shot Mom the finger. For everyone to see. Big and bad."

CASS

Cicadas? My head pounded so hard and loud I didn't know if the sound was inside or out. Dark all around, but white noise. Go figure.

"Hey, are you asleep or dead?"

Kyle.

Not cicadas. Not white noise. Static from the radio. He was back. Oh thank god, he was back. How long had he been gone? Was it night or day? Was it Sunday now? Had I been asleep? Could it be Monday? Had it just been minutes? Time was impossible here. I faded in and out, sentences paused and I didn't know if it was seconds and minutes or . . .

I moved my thumb to the button. Even that was an effort. I pressed. Opened my mouth to speak. It was already open, my tongue swollen and the tip sticking out between my front teeth a bit. Stuck to the top of my mouth. I tried to talk but my tongue was foreign, too heavy and cumbersome. All I managed was a rusty groan. Even breathing seemed to take grueling effort. I was going to die. That thought wasn't panic now. It was truth.

"Miserable down there?"

I groaned again. Not part of my campaign. Reactive. I couldn't think or plan with this headache or tongue or all-encompassing thirst. I brought my left hand to my lips to break the scab on my knuckles and lick the blood, but a sweet, sick liquid oozed out. Pus? Wounds get infected that quickly? Why couldn't I have learned a few facts in biology classes? I sighed. Like it would help to know what was going to kill me first: infection, dehydration, or the cold.

I worked my tongue loose from my hard palate and tried to own it. I pressed the button again. "Water, please, water."

A lot of nothing from Kyle. Then, "You sound like crap."

A lot of nothing from me.

"Okay, but only because I'm not done with you

yet." The silver dollar–sized circle of light appeared above me. It hurt my eyes and I turned my head away. It hurt to move. God, it hurt to move.

"Try to get your mouth under here and I'll pour water down the tube. I've got a quart bottle and I'll give you half. That's all."

I shifted and opened my mouth. Waited. Water trickled down. Onto my nose. I wriggled up, lapping at the spillage, and then opening for the dribbling stream that dropped onto my tongue. I soaked in the water rather than drank it, my tongue taking it in like a reverse sponge, shrinking as it absorbed, then water oozed into my mouth and finally down my throat, wetting it. I only swallowed two or three times before the trickle eased then stopped.

It wouldn't save my body from dehydrating, but I could talk again. Kyle won this skirmish. He won it big.

If I worked it hard enough, I might be able to get more water, but that would cede him even more power. I couldn't afford that. I knew to keep the endgame in mind. No short-term wins. Get out of the box. Get out of this box.

Then kick his ass.

The light flicked away. But not before I caught a glimpse of myself in the dim glow. I'd worried about pee stains? My white pj's were dirt streaked, the knees torn out and bloodied. My guess was that the elbows were in the same shape since I could feel the pain of scrapes there. My fingers and knuckles were in worse shape than I'd imagined from the feel. And the feel was shredded. My right thumb was in good shape. Taped securely to the button of the radio. Stiff, yes, but unbloodied. I wanted out of here with enough strength left to take a swing at this guy, with the radio still taped to my hand.

I had been chasing a thought before. What was it? I couldn't think. I drummed my heels against the wood. Pain. Something wet, slippery. Blood?

The pain brought me back into focus a bit. Kyle. If I was here because I hurt his brother and he was this protector/avenger guy, then why hadn't I ever known about a brother? I had kept tabs on Kyle when I was a freshman. If they were close, I would have seen them together, *something*.

Why was David such a secret?

Did Kyle treat David like a creeping fungus and now he felt guilty?

But there was Monster Mom.

Did he have to protect David on the sly to keep Monster Mom on his side? To keep her from leaving him the way the dad already had?

And if he was Kyle the protector and he and David were close, the question I wanted answered was *why me*? If David Kirby was the kind to go suicidal from rejection, why would he ask *me* for a date? And why would Kyle let him? It's not like I have a rep for taking in strays.

Once at a party I told my date to get me another drink, and he said, "Sure, Your Bitchness." The place went quiet and people kind of gaped. I didn't miss a beat. "That's your Royal Bitchness, peasant, and bow when you say it." Sure, there was the head tilt, grin, and twinking to make it golden, but . . .

What tender heart would lay himself open to me? If David's stupid enough to try, am I supposed to know he's walking around with a noose hanging from his neck looking for a convenient branch?

I might be dying, but I was going to die angry.

THIS.

WASN'T.

MY.

FAULT.

It was time to take Kyle to the table and close the deal.

"You've had your water; can you talk now?"

"I can talk." I said it soft, but firm, taking back my position. "The question is, are you listening?"

Nothing.

Then, "What's that mean?"

"I'll get back to it. First, I've got the big question for you. Why am I here? Don't give me your shit about David and my note. That's an excuse; that's not a reason. Why did David ask me out? *Me.* I bet David didn't get to me by himself."

I pulled down to regretful and sad. I didn't want Kyle on the defensive. "So, do you have the guts to get real and tell the truth before you kill me?"

The silence went on so long, I wondered if he left. If I had pushed the wrong button, pushed it too hard.

"He didn't get to you by himself. I led him."

I almost didn't hear it. It sounded like something he had just admitted to himself.

I had to close my eyes to concentrate. If I opened them, there were weird dancing *things* in front of me. Not lights, but sort of muted color, shadowy spots that flicked and flittered.

He had clicked off the radio and I felt him pacing across the ground over me. I sensed he was reaching critical mass. He needed another nudge.

Pulling the walkie close to my mouth and clicking the button felt like it took a year. Things swirled and whirled and I drummed my heels again so the pain would keep me from passing out. "What do you mean?"

He popped the walkie to life, but waited a long time to talk. Or was time going tilty?

"This year Mom started in on David about the gay thing. 'Why don't you date? You never have a girlfriend. You've never gone on a single date. I think you're queer. That's it. I've got a sissy boy on my hands. My whole life was ruined by a little pervert.'

"David would call asking me what to do. I admit, I was sick of the calls. Couldn't I have a life of my

176

own without David pulling me back into that horror show all the time? I'd tell him to let her blow off steam, to just stay out of her way. Quit making yourself such a target, I told him.

"But he said she followed him around the house, screaming like a maniac, nagging and sniping at him. She was pissed because his grades were bad. She'd spew at him about being gay, not having dates, and ruining her life. Over and over.

"And that's where you came in," Kyle said.

Something was wrong with me. Really bad wrong. My legs were twitching and Kyle was fading in and out, syncing with the lights behind my eyes that dimmed then glared. The pounding in my head kept the backbeat. No matter how Zen I tried to go, my breath was coming fast, shallow but rapid. On TV hospital dramas, that's never good news.

"Hey, what's with you?"

"Sorry." I sounded like a sick frog. I tried to slide my tongue over my lips. Like a nail file over rocks. "How did I get in the picture?"

"If David got a date with someone — not just any someone, but someone Mom would approve of — she would back off. How could she come down on him if he dangled a pretty girl in front of her?"

I heard expelled air in the radio. It hurt my ears and made my head roar. "I told him just what he had to look for, the type. She had to be like Mom. She had to be . . . it had to be someone that was so much like her that she had to think David finally stepped up. She would give him her approval if he picked her clone for a date. God, I was such a moron."

It took me a minute. Because my synapses were dying or because no one wants to see their ugly side?

"That's why he picked me," I whispered. My eyes burned but there were no tears there.

"I'm her. I'm your mother."

BEN

Ben's first impression of the woman at the door was that she might have been pretty once. Before disappointment hardened her face into angles and points.

She backed away, gesturing them in, and then preceded them into a large room, leaving Scott to close the door. Seating herself in the middle of the couch, she didn't ask the men to sit.

Ben knew a power play when presented with one and sat in a leather club chair and pointed Scott toward another. Mrs. Kirby crossed her legs.

"David's case is closed. It was ruled a suicide."

"I understand that, Mrs. Kirby. Detective Michaels and I are sorry for your loss and don't intrude on your time lightly. But, there's been a kidnapping, and we need some information from you and we'd like to talk to your son Kyle."

"Kyle." She waved dismissively. "Who knows where he is? He's been in and out. Mostly out. I can't keep track. We mourn differently. He does everything alone."

Ben stared down at his notebook. How had the investigating officer characterized her? A piece of work?

"Mrs. Kirby, did David know Cass McBride?"

She laughed. Or barked. Ben wasn't quite sure what it was.

"For pity's sake. If you had known David – Stop, if you even had gotten a good look at him, you'd . . . well, you'd know how laughable . . ."

She smoothed a nonexistent wrinkle in her slacks. "I'm quite certain David knew who Cass McBride is. Even I know who she is. Rich, pretty – her picture is in the local newspaper regularly. But would she know David? She wouldn't give him the time of day. No girl like that would."

Ben's spine stiffened and Scott's mouth gaped slightly open.

"David was — well, what some would call less than desirable," she continued. She turned to the men and ran the fingers of her right hand through her hair, massaging the temples, then down to the nape of her neck, rubbing. "Bless his heart."

When she noticed Ben's stiff posture, she pulled her hand away from her neck and looked directly at him. "You're not used to honesty, are you? No one is. Everyone thinks I'm heartless. But I'm simply honest. David was a timid boy, and he wasn't tough enough for this world. He quit everything he started. I'm not surprised he quit his life. I *am* surprised at the violent way he did it, though."

Ben thought the tendons in her neck would snap.

"Kyle is off being traumatized somewhere, my husband is just off somewhere, and here I am, holding down the fort alone. As always."

Ben wished he could tell Scott to close his gaping mouth. Sure, this woman was shocking the squat out of him too. Her son hadn't been dead a week and she was — well, Ben guessed it didn't matter how long the kid had been dead.

"Does Kyle know Cass?"

"That would be more in line," she said. "But he's never mentioned her."

"Would you mind if we had a look at Kyle's closet? His shoes?"

Mrs. Kirby's self-pity took a sharp turn. "Seriously? What the hell are you up to?"

KYLE

"I told Cass all about her, you know. My mother."

The young cop had been pacing, but now he sat down. The big cop was still leading me with silence.

"The first time I saw Cass, I hated her, because I thought she had it all. But when word went around school that her dad divorced her mom and left her without a cent . . ."

My thumb was bleeding again. I tugged the sleeves back over my hand.

"See, once I met Cass's dad and then heard how he treated her mom, I thought what a bitch she must be to stay and live with him. She either had to be just like him, or she'd sell her soul to stay on his pay-check."

I looked up at the big cop. "Have you met her

father?" The cop didn't give me anything but I kept talking. "I met him once. He sold Mom her car. Shit. I can't believe it. How much my mom and Cass's dad are alike. With Cass's dad it's sales and with my mother it's torture, but it works the same way. Keeping the prize dangling just out of reach. If the sale is too easy, you can walk away. . . .

"When I walked away from Cass, I told myself that I was through with her. I wanted her to know she was there because of what she did to David. To understand what a bitch she was and to suffer in that box. To go out of her mind with fear. But I ended up spilling my guts. I left because I knew she was getting to me. But now it's like a lightbulb going off in my head. Her dad is a version of my mom. Both snakes, but Mom has venom; he's a constrictor."

I rubbed my face again. *Hmmmm, I wonder if her mother is a doormat like my dad?*

"The craziest part of this entire thing is . . . as much as I still hate her, even if she had all the reason in the world to hate me, Cass, she gave me all the answers.

"I know it sounds weird, but . . . I kind of liked talking to her."

CASS

I wanted to scream; I wanted to come out of that box just to slap his stupid, stupid face. But I was too tired to raise my voice above a croak. The disco lights that danced on my eyelids were fading and I was sleepy. My head was as cottony as my mouth, but one thing was clear — I was in here for all the wrong reasons.

Kyle wasn't even mad at me.

"When you figure this out, you're . . . well, I don't know how you'll feel about it," I said.

"What's that supposed to mean?"

"It means that you've got it all wrong. You don't want *me* in this box. I'm not the problem. If you want to feel better, feel like you've avenged your brother, then torture the person who tortured your brother — go get your *mother* and put her in this box. That woman shit on your brother every day of his life. She wouldn't even feed her kid. Her own child. Did you really understand that note? If David blamed me, he would have pinned my note to his body too. Right?"

Nothing.

I had to keep talking. The buzz in my head was piercing. A band saw chewing up my skull. I had to get this out now because I knew I didn't have any time left.

"David's note was aimed straight for your mother. Her words are teeth. He wants her to feed on his corpse. He hung himself in your *front* yard. He wanted people to know, to *know* what she did to him."

Still nothing.

"If I die and she lives — how does that make you feel better? She wins even bigger that way."

More nothing.

And then the radio clicked off. I heard a long, anguished howl. Loud enough to vibrate through the earth.

And then he was gone.

I knew he was gone. I could feel it.

This was all — backward or sideways or . . . I couldn't think, my head hurt and this fading in and out kept me from focusing. What did I do wrong? I had it all figured out . . . I knew what I . . .

Oh shit.

I'd done part of it right. I'd convinced him that burying me was covering up the problem. And covering up the problem, never letting it come to light, was how his mother got away with wounding David with her words until she bled him dry.

But I was supposed to make Kyle see that his mother always made sure someone else paid the price for her shortcomings, for her mistakes. Kyle was supposed to dig me up so I wouldn't die for what his mother had done to David.

I was supposed to convince him that his mother murdered David.

And she couldn't make Kyle responsible for murdering me.

He was supposed to get me out *first*.

Now he was gone.

I wasn't supposed to . . . I didn't think he'd self-destruct . . . I . . . didn't . . .

I signed my own death certificate.

My eyes are closed. I own the dark now. I can hear my heartbeat in my ears and it's got a flutter or maybe I mean a stutter. I'm too weak to bang my heels, my breath kind of rattles, and my tongue has gotten thick again. The things that should hurt, my shredded fingers and toes and heels, don't. The places where I've bitten through my lips and where they've cracked and bled, none of that hurts. But I'm cold and I shiver and jerk and that makes my joints feel like they are grinding. And my head. Pounding, buzzing, the whirling lights.

BEN

Ben sat at his desk, fingers laced behind his head, feet on the desk, concentrating on the crime board, staring at the names, the facts, trying to make sense or order, trying to will something to jump out at him.

"First forty-eight are over. I hate to lose and our chances of winning are . . ." He didn't want to say it.

"We keep looking," Roger said. He printed NEW DRUG on the board in green ink. "The lab said the sheets did show drug traces, but it's a mix they aren't familiar with. They're talking to people to see what's new out there. If it's new, we have a better chance of seeing who has access."

"I'm tired." Ben kneaded the back of his neck

and pulled his feet down. "I haven't slept since who-knows-how long and all the pistons aren't firing. I know I'm missing something." He stared at the board again.

Scott drummed the desktop. "Ben?"

"Scott, stop with the noise. I hate repetitive noises. You know I hate —"

Roger grinned, thinking of Ben's own finger-drumming habit.

"Ben." Scott still drummed, seeming not to hear Ben's complaint.

"What, Scott?"

"Who has access to new drugs on the market?"

"I dunno, docs, pharmacists? Roger, do you — oh, that's it!"

Scott rose and headed for the board. "Pharmaceutical reps get the new stuff that's out and they peddle it to the docs. Right? That's what they do?"

"And the Kirby kid's father is a rep," Roger said. "But David died before Cass was snatched."

Scott drew a red line from Kyle's name to Cass's.

"The brother," Ben said. "But we checked his shoes. Right size, no tread match, no glass cuts."

"We didn't check the ones he was wearing," Scott said.

"And he's been out more than in," Ben added. "Let's get back to the Kirby house and shake something loose."

KYLE

"I got in my truck and floored it all the way home. I grabbed some rope from the back; there's always stuff like that in my truck. I didn't want to bury her. I wanted to hang her from that tree, let the neighbors see her out there. Dad was gone, of course, and I slammed in through the front door and went into the kitchen and grabbed one of the big knives out of the block on the counter.

"Mom was already yelling. Calling out, asking if that was me. Screaming that she had a headache and couldn't I be a little considerate." I stopped.

I dug my nails into my thumbs again. This time I didn't care if they saw me bleed. "You know what, a real killer would have heard her voice and turned around and run away. He'd figure he couldn't kill something that sounded like that without a silver bullet and a stake to the heart."

I looked at the big cop. "I know how that sounds. Blame the gene pool."

"Keep going, Kyle. You're almost done."

I stormed up the stairs and jerked her out of bed.

"What the hell do you think you're —"

I shoved the tip of the knife under her chin. "Shut your mouth. Just shut up before I kill you or I'll cut your tongue out."

She clamped her mouth shut. I didn't think I'd ever see it. Mom alive and not talking. David and I were certain she even talked in her sleep. I pushed the tip of the knife a little harder so it pierced the skin just under her chin and a dot of blood appeared.

"So you can bleed? I wasn't sure you were human. You know what I just figured out, Mom? You murdered David." She opened her mouth and I pushed the knife harder; the spot turned into a trickle. She gulped out a little scream of pain. Tears ran down her cheeks.

"Yes, you talked him to death. You ranted and screamed and bullied him until he had no hope left. And you know what? Dad let you. And even worse, I let you. You killed him and we watched. You tore hunks out of him day after day until there was nothing left."

She sagged, so I cranked her arm around behind her and pulled up, putting the knife across her throat. "And why? Not because you hated him. Because you're a mean, horrible woman and you don't know how to do anything. You don't even know how to be decent."

I stopped a minute as a phrase floated into my head. "You chop other people up so you can feel whole."

I shoved her back with my shoulder. "Now we're going outside. And the whole world is going to see what a rotten piece of shit you are."

I tried to force her down the stairs. She was screaming and fighting me. She kicked me and jerked back and went tumbling down the steps.

"That's when you guys came in."

I dropped my head. Chin to chest. Exhausted. "I don't know what else you want me to say. But I want a

194

trial. I want it all real public. You cheated me out of hanging my mother out for people to see, but I still want it to happen.

"I'm done talking. Until the trial."

CASS

Is he coming back?
He has to come back.
My only way out is through him.
He has to let me out of here.
Kyle, he's the only one . . .
Kyle has to . . .
Kyle . . .
I can't get out if Kyle doesn't . . .
I can't if Kyle doesn't . . .

BEN

Ben pulled into the Kirby driveway. His headlights flooded the front of the house. He pointed to the front door. Not ajar. Wide open. Almost midnight; the only light on was upstairs and the door was wide open. Not good.

Ben picked up the radio and called for backup, turned off the car, and glanced at Scott.

Scott nodded and unholstered his weapon. A .357. The young ones always carried a cannon.

Ben motioned Scott to the back and approached the open door from the side.

Standing between the door and a window, Ben eased over to check the front room. Nothing. Where was backup?

A scream sounded from the house. Ben braced

his gun hand and stuck his Glock around the door-jamb to draw fire.

None.

"No!" A thud. More screaming. More thuds. Like someone falling down the stairs.

Ben stepped into the house, gun up and braced; he heard the back door open. Scott.

"One more scream and I'll slit your throat." Male voice. Young.

Ben sidestepped down the entry hall. The hall turned and opened out to the stairs.

A young man stood over Mrs. Kirby, who lay in a tangled heap at the foot of the stairs. Her body was stiff but her eyes were wild with terror. The young man held a large kitchen knife to her throat. A nylon rope was on the floor beside her.

"Police. Drop your weapon."

The young man looked up, his eyes glazed with fatigue, and blind rage and disgust.

"Don't stop me. You can shoot me after if you want to. But don't stop me. I have to do this. I have to."

"Drop your weapon, son," Ben said.

"I don't want to just slit her throat. Don't make me do that. It's not enough."

"Calm down," Ben said. He wanted the boy to look at him. He needed him to turn his head a little. Scott should be coming in from the back, easing through the kitchen.

"Let's see what's happening here," Ben said.

The kid looked at him. "Go away. Either shoot me or get out."

Scott moved in. Ben shifted. The kid shifted with him. Holding his mother's hair in one hand, her head tipped back, the knife resting across the jugular, he kept his eyes on Ben's gun.

"I don't like those options." Ben shifted again, pulling the young man around, his back more to Scott. "I've met Mrs. Kirby. I'm thinking you're Kyle. You look a lot like your mother. I'm guessing you don't want to hear that right now, though.

"She's not worth the trouble you're going to put yourself in. Drop your weapon and let's work something out." He shifted again.

And quicker than a snake strike, Scott's foot was under Kyle's elbow, kicking up and out, the knife flying toward the wall. Ben's gun was against Kyle's temple.

"Let go of your mother's hair."

Kyle released his mother. She scrambled to her feet, almost spitting. "What the fuck do you —" Before she could kick her son, Scott grabbed Mrs. Kirby. Roger and Tyrell pounded in.

Ben cuffed Kyle and pulled him to a sitting position. "Put her somewhere. Take a statement. Take her to the hospital if she needs it. But keep her away from here," Ben said.

He turned back to Kyle, did a full Miranda, and then squatted down to get eye to eye.

"You're in a world of trouble."

"Why did you come here?" Kyle asked. "You were here before she screamed. The neighbors couldn't have called."

"I think you have something to do with Cass McBride's disappearance."

The kid dropped his head. Ben was amazed.

There was no show of anger or defiance or even a try at innocence.

"Yeah, I took her," Kyle said.

"What did you do with her?" Ben asked.

"I buried her. When I left her she was alive. But I doubt she is now."

CASS

How much time?
Have I been asleep?
My tongue is thicker than before.
It's so hard to breathe.
But the pounding
in my head . . .
is not so loud
anymore.
And
the whirling lights
are

getting

dimmer.

BEN

It took fifteen minutes of tire-squealing, limit-busting driving to reach the greenhouse. But the kid's directions were precise. An ambulance and a van with shovels and people to use them were on the way.

Ben was out of the car before it was completely still. It was dark, but he had aimed the headlights at the door. He found the switch, and row upon row of fluorescent or grow lights buzzed into life.

"There!" Scott shouted, pointing at a rectangle of disturbed dirt.

Grave-sized.

Scott whirled around, caught sight of a small hand spade. He grabbed it and began digging at the loose earth. Ben saw a shovel leaning against the back wall, but heard the van roar up. He waved the shovel — carrying cops into the greenhouse. They headed to Scott and dug. Hard and efficient.

Ben found what appeared to be a vacuum cleaner hose protruding from the disturbed earth. He knelt down and picked it up. Snapped off the filter cap. "Cass, can you hear me?"

"Cass?"

Scott got out of the way of the big shovels. He gave Ben a questioning look. He turned and went to the other end of the grave. Another hose stuck out. It was duct-taped to a big funnel. Taped into the funnel was a computer fan, which was hooked to a part of a computer box, and the whole thing was hooked to a long string of extension cords that ran to an electrical receptacle.

"Damn! Clever, simple, easy to make, easy to get parts, quiet, and gets the job done." Scott waved at Ben and pointed to the device. "It won't move a lot of air, there's got to be some carbon dioxide buildup, but she's got a chance, right?"

"I can't hear anything," Ben said. "Cass, Cass, wake up. Come on, Cass. I'm Ben Gray and I'm here to help you. A lot of people are here to help you. We're going to get you out of there. But I want you to say something. Talk to me. Okay. Try to say something, Cass. People say you're the girl that gets things done. So, say something, Cass."

One of the paramedics leaned in to Ben. He spoke quickly, pointing to a clear tube he was holding and then to the one Ben had.

"Got it," Ben said.

He returned to the air tube. "Cass, the paramedic is going to run an oxygen tube down this one, so I won't be talking to you for a minute and a clear tube will poke out at you in just a few seconds. Then we'll pump some oxygen down. It's going to perk you up a little. Just breathe deep when it comes in. Then talk to me, Cass. Please. Say something."

Ben handed the tube to the waiting paramedic.

"Tube's in." He passed the tube back to Ben and whirled his finger in the air. "Okay, oxygen's pumping. Nobody smokes in here."

"Cass?"

Ben rubbed his head. "Can't you guys dig faster?"

"Why didn't we get the walkie from the kid?" Scott said.

"It's in the front seat of his truck. Still at his house," Ben said. He put the tube up to his ear. "I think I hear her breathing."

"That's the oxygen, Detective," the paramedic said. At Ben's bitter glance, he looked away and muttered, "Sorry."

"Cass, we've got him. Kyle can't hurt you again, so don't be afraid. Tell me you're alive, Cass. Talk to me. C'mon, Cass. Be the girl that wins."

"We're here. There's a tarp over the box."

"Get that off," Ben barked.

Scott dropped to his stomach and grabbed the tarp, pulling it back with him.

Crowbars replaced shovels and the box lid was levered up.

Ben looked in.

"Jesus," he said.

CASS

I'm back in a dark, narrow space with a square button under my thumb. Talking. Finding the words for my story. I do this every night.

I know I'm not still in the box. After all the lights went dim, I woke up and was in the hospital.

The hospital spooked me — so loud and busy and glaring. Sensory overload. I pulled blankets over my head. If anyone pulled them away, I shook and whimpered until someone took pity and returned the blankets.

I think I slept a lot. Tranquilizers? Don't know. Don't care. Sleep was good. Dark, restful, and quiet. I woke once and Dad was holding my right hand. The one that had held the radio. My left hand was in bandages that looked like a boxing glove. My feet looked the same way.

He seemed to sense my eyes open, or he was watching. But he looked straight at me and started crying. I closed my eyes again and went back to sleep, but I don't think he let go.

Later, I woke up because I felt something move the bed. Weight near me. I woke up a little more fully and saw my mother. This time it was me that started crying. She pulled me into her arms and I nuzzled my face into her neck like I used to do when I was a little kid. She stroked my hair and said, "I hear you. I hear you, Bebe. You don't have to say a word."

Do unspoken words speak loudest? Say the most?

A big man came to see me and said he had been the lead detective on my case. He said I talked my way out of that grave. That might be true. But he's ignoring something.

I talked my way into it.

When I realized that, I decided to start listening.

So I've stopped talking to people. It's not that I

can't talk. I think that I don't know when I should talk and when I shouldn't.

Sometime later, I was transferred to the psych unit. I like it here. Safe and quiet. My doctor says that I did die in that grave. A person doesn't really live through something like that. A new person is born and steps out.

My fingers and toes aren't in bandages anymore. They told me I had skin grafts because they were shredded to the bone. My fingertips are all patchy and funky-looking.

But how did I heal so quickly? Nothing is making sense. What people say, things, time; it's still all mixed up.

For instance, Mom was here today. She told me that Dad bought her a house so she can stay here with me. Bought the furniture, but let her pick it all out herself. That's as reasonable as me saying I'll go home with Mom and live in the swamp and sling crawfish and take in foster children and never be a bitch. Get serious. Dad might buy her a house to stay near me after all this mess, but he'd never, ever let her pick out the furniture. So that other stuff is probably wrong too.

My mother has brought Christmas trees here. Little ones, all decorated, to "cheer up my room for the season," she says. And presents. And she and Dad have both brought birthday presents. And cakes. More than once.

Why all that in just a few months? Are they just trying to make me think time has passed so I'll get better sooner?

I don't care how many cakes or Christmas trees come in here. I know it's only been a few months because I haven't been called to testify at the trial.

Kyle's.

Detective Gray came back to tell me that if I was afraid of Kyle, I didn't have to be. Kyle was in prison. He wasn't even in general population, but in a special section. He has a cell to himself. Kyle spends all his time with law books, trying to find a way to put his mother in jail for being responsible for David's murder.

The shrink wonders if I have some sort of Stockholm syndrome. You know, like I bonded or fell in love with Kyle. That's not this movie. I get it that Kyle lived with a monster, but he had choices, and someone that buries a human being alive should be locked up forever.

And that's where the time thing goes all — wrong. I know Kyle can't be in prison yet. I know there hasn't been a trial. The only way out of that box was through Kyle. And the only way to get Kyle in prison was through me. I had to put him there. I had to go to that trial and testify. Tell the story. How could anyone know what happened if I didn't tell them? He put me in my box, and I have to be the one to put him in his.

At night I crawl into the narrow metal locker in my room with a tape recorder held in my right hand. I punch the button with my thumb and I tell the story. I start from the beginning when David asked me out to the end where I'm making the tape. Here in the dark where there's no place to hide from myself. And then I listen.

And then I erase.

And when the words make sense and all the blame is where it belongs, I'll be ready to talk in the light.

Acknowledgments

As ever to my wonderful agent, Scott Treimel, for taking such good care of me. To Andrea Spooner, my editor, who gave me a shovel, taught me to dig and did it so graciously. To Sangeeta Mehta, the assistant editor that kept us both sane. Deb Vanasse, thanks for the early read and catching the big inconsistency. Pam Whitlock for listening to me read this thing over and over when she should have been resting.

And to the memory of my most steadfast writing companion, Jack London, my Great Pyrenees, who sat by my feet through every revision of every book I've had published right through this one. Yes, I'm aware he was a dog, but he was my muse and my companion, and he wouldn't let me out of my chair until I was finished. I miss him.

And to Little, Brown — thanks for having me.

GAIL GILES might not be claustrophobic, but she was inspired to write *What Happened to Cass McBride* when she was snowbound at home in Alaska. "I was entombed," she remembers, "and I felt like I was buried alive. And then I knew I had to write about what that experience might be like." Gail is also the acclaimed author of *Playing in Traffic*, *Dead Girls Don't Write Letters*, and *Shattering Glass* (an American Library Association Best of the Best selection). She now lives in The Woodlands, Texas, with her husband, her cat, and two dogs. She blogs at notjazz.livejournal.com.

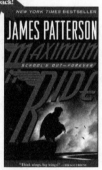

1) At first glance, the title *What Happened to Cass McBride?* seems to refer to Cass's disappearance, meaning, "Where is Cass McBride?" But the title may have other implications as well. For example, what happened to Cass emotionally a) after she learned of David's suicide, b) after she realized she had been buried alive, c) when she found a way to get through to Kyle, and d) when she awoke in the hospital? Perhaps the title asks, "How did this experience change Cass as a person?" How do you think some of the characters (such as Kyle, Cass's dad, and her friend Erica) might answer this question?

2) Ben describes the McBride home as "a place of barely beige and white, chrome and glass. Cold. Nothing could feel at home here but ghosts." Do you think Cass felt at home there? How do you think the pale colors of Cass's room and clothes might be a reflection of her character? When she recovers, do you think Cass will still dress in white? How do you think she might redecorate her room?

3) This book gives a great deal of attention to parent-child relationships. How is Cass's relationship with her father similar to Kyle's relationship with his mother? Do you believe that Cass's father thinks about her differently in the end? Cass uncharacteristically wrote in ink in an Emily Dickinson book of poetry that had "a bunch of stuff about fathers" in it. What do you think Cass might have written in the book?

4) In this book, words are weapons. By taping a walkie-talkie to Cass's hand and confining her in a box, Kyle is able to "torture" Cass by talking to her—and forcing her to talk to him—as she dies. What methods does Cass use to save herself through talking? What would you have said to Kyle that Cass didn't say?

5) In addition to acting as weapons, words can serve as a defense as well, allowing characters to justify their actions. Kyle wants the world to know his story, and Cass wants to testify against Kyle. Do you think it is most important to have the opportunity to tell your story, or do you agree with Cass when she ponders in the end, "Do unspoken words speak loudest? Say the most?" Can you think of instances in the book when a character's silence has revealed something important about him or her that words could not have?

6) How do you think the balance of power between Kyle and Cass would have been different if he had held her in a room instead of underground and they had interacted face-to-face? Do you think it would've been easier for Cass to escape? Why do you think Kyle decided to bury her instead of "torturing" her another way?

7) When Cass awoke in the box, she screamed in terror "until [she] felt like the blood vessels in [her] face and neck would burst." Still, at the end, Cass is recording her story in a dark, cramped locker. She seems more comfortable in this coffin-like space than in the well-lit hospital. How do you think Cass's fear has shifted by the end of the novel? What has Cass gained and lost through her fear? Why do you think she erases the tape before letting anyone listen to it? In the end, do you

believe Cass is broken?

8) Kyle is a scary figure because of his ability to discon-
nect himself from the person he is hurting (Cass) while
he blames another (his mother). Yet, Kyle is vulnerable,
too. Cass notes, "Kyle *was* struggling. His emotions were
frayed and close to the surface. . . . Weakness." What are
Kyle's biggest "weaknesses"? How do they make him
more approachable, but more dangerous at the same
time? What do you think scares Kyle most?

9) Revenge is a strong focus of the book: David kills
himself to get revenge on those who wouldn't accept
him; Kyle buries Cass because she rejected David; Kyle's
mother verbally abuses her children because she blames
them for her unhappy life; Kyle tries to kill his mother
after years of coping with abuse; Cass wants to help
convict Kyle. How do you think the course of events
might have changed if some of the characters were able
to forgive one another? Do you think, in the end,
anyone is forgiven?

10) Cass closes the novel with, "And when the words make sense and all the blame is where it belongs, I'll be ready to talk in the light." How does blame shift in the novel? Where do you think the blame belongs? Which character(s) do you think would agree with you?